Those

Who Wander

The Puzzle Box
Chronicles: Book 3

Those Who Wander

Shawn P. McCarthy

The Puzzle Box Chronicles
Book 3

Dark Spark Press

Book cover design by Teodora Chinde
Printed in the United States of America
First Printing, 2016
ISBN-13: 978-0-9968967-4-0 (Dark Spark Press)
ISBN-10: 0-9968967-4-0

Dark Spark Press

      www.DarkSparkPress.com

      Publisher.DarkSparkPress@gmail.com

For

My Sisters

Debbie, Laurel, & Eileen

Chapter 1

Losses

July, 1891

Summer winds can carry a bitter smell.

Hot days become a catalyst. The old biology breaks down and new life rises from decay. Aromas burst forth from a million chemical reactions and the present consumes the past.

Such aromas are particularly noticeable in big cities. On warm Boston evenings, a bitter fragrance is stirred by breezes pulled in off the ocean, mixing a slight salty scent into a perfume that includes horses, food, people and factory smoke.

But there is also the sweetness of new flowers.

The lingering oak pollen.

The garbage that floats in the bay, pushed along by natural eddies.

And there are other fleeting scents known mostly to those who lie low in the evenings, down near the grass, amongst the June bugs and grasshoppers. It's a sugary smell. A fresh perfume sent to mask the musk of the simmering city.

This evening, Amanda Grant (formerly Amanda Malcom) smells this secondary smell and closes her eyes. It carries hints from childhood. Playing in open spaces, sitting outside on the evenings shucking peas or frolicking on the lawn. She remembers mothers gathering around an outdoor table to do their quilting.

Down next to the grass the world is different. Here, on the lawn of the Boston Common, she lies low, stretched out, gazing at the clouds. She is closer to the warm earth than she's been in years. The grass tickles the back of her neck. Happiness settles in.

There is a rustle beside her on the ground – Jeb Thomas rises to take a peach from their picnic basket. He leans his head well away from his white shirt as he bites into it, juice dribbling through his fingers and adding to the scents. Then he lies back down beside her.

A peaceful time for a pair of new friends.

They both scan for shapes hidden in the clouds. So far they've seen a cow, a man's hat, a snow bank, and something Jeb claimed was a pine tree, but which Amanda thought looked like a dog's wagging tail.

"How's the peach?" she asks.

"Sweeter than it has any right to be."

He winks at her and they both laugh.

"You know what *is* funny?" Amanda asks. She thinks about taking his hand as she talks, but decides not to rush toward intimacy. This is only their third meeting. Current

Boston etiquette dictates that a woman should not move that fast.

"What?" Jeb asks, turning on his side and propping his head against his elbow.

"I think it's funny how different my life has become, in such a short time."

"Well, you did leave your husband. I guess you knew it was going to be different."

"Yes. But it's more than that." She sits up and takes a peach of her own. "When I was a girl, I would never have accompanied a boy or man on a picnic like this. Certainly not without a proper escort. You do know what people would have thought. Instead, someone, maybe a brother, an aunt or a neighbor, would have come with us. We all would have sat together making small talk. Whoever the escort was, he or she would have been watching and evaluating right along with me to see if you're worth my time."

Jeb chuckles. "Ah, well, good thing you don't have an escort then. I don't think I could handle the pressure."

Amanda holds her peach directly in front of Jeb so that he can take a bite. But as he gets close, she slowly pulls it back, making him follow it until he grabs her arm and sinks his teeth into the sweet pulp.

"Proper courting for a proper woman, isn't that what people expect?" Amanda asks. "Yet here I am. Alone on a picnic with a single man. It's all perfectly innocent. We're in a public park with a hundred other people. Yet we're lacking discretion in some people's eyes."

Jeb looks around at the other people wandering through the Common. "I guess that's true. But I don't see one solitary soul looking at us, do you? No one knows us here. No one cares one whit about who we are or why we're here. Maybe they think we're married. And if they don't, they probably don't care. It's our business, not theirs. Isn't that wonderful?"

Amanda looks around and slowly nods. "In some ways yes, it is. But has society changed so much in the last three years? Did something happen while I was married?"

He shrugs. "Probably not. I think it's probably you that changed. Decorum and etiquette may have lost their allure."

Amanda playfully pushes him, then lies back again to study the evening clouds. A tall and a small cloud roll by, looking like a child chasing after a ball.

Is it change that she senses? Or does she simply misunderstand what the world expects from her? She once placed such importance on appearances and how she was expected to act. But recent history has taught her that most of the men and women don't care about her at all. They don't even think about her. They nod hello and then go about their business. It's a nice feeling. The vague acceptance of others is a side of city life that she's learning to enjoy.

"You were sweet to pack a supper for us," Jeb declares. "It's nice for me to get away from the rooming house. Does it feel good for you to get out, too?"

"It does indeed. And since I couldn't exactly invite you over for tea, a little supper on the ground was really our only choice."

"Oh?"

"Yes. It's a bit awkward at the Morgans' these days. They're pretty much waiting for me to leave."

"I see," he says while nibbling on a piece of white cheese. "And where will you go?"

"That's a good question. I'm not really sure. I've been looking for jobs in the row of shops a few blocks from here, but they're hard to come by. Plus, it would be tough to earn enough there for room and board. I've even thought about being a maid, just to have a place to live. But … well, I don't know."

"I don't see you as the maid type at all," Jeb laughs.

"Want to hear something crazy? I've also thought that maybe I should find some way that I could travel."

This seems to spark Jeb's interest. "Well, why don't you?"

"Well," she says with a devilish grin, "I just might. You travel quite a bit and you seem to like it. So here's what I've thought. Promise you won't laugh?"

"Cross my heart. Though I could use a good laugh, believe me."

She sits up, crossing her legs as best she can in her restrictive dress. "Okay, here's what I've been thinking. I've thought about trying to get a job on a train. You know, work on there. Sleep on there. Eat. Everything! And as the train moves, I get to see new places. I get to see the side of America I've only read about."

"Oh, come on," Jeb replies. She can tell he wants to be supportive, but that he has his doubts. "It's mostly men who work on the trains."

"Yes. Mostly. But there are some women, too. Car maids and such."

"They're called porters, not maids. And they're pretty much men. Mostly negro men."

"No, silly, I'm not talking about the porters. I'm talking about actual maids. Maids who work in private railcars and travel with families."

Jeb is silent for a moment, mulling over the idea.

"If I'm going to take a job as a lowly maid, I'm at least going to get one that allows me to do something else I've wanted to do at the same time." She tips her head to try to catch his eyes. "Now tell me … doesn't that seem like an interesting way to combine travel and work?"

Jeb pulls a piece of grass from the ground and separates it, pulling the sweet stem from its base. He tucks the piece between his teeth, chewing it slightly. "It's creative, I guess. But hell, seeing the country isn't what you think. People like you and me, most of what we see out there are the things we'll never have. Every state has its big houses. But you can never see the inside of them. Every city has its big buildings, but you're not welcome there. I've been back and forth across America at least five times. And you know what I've seen that I like the best? What I like is what folks have right around here. The houses and the small villages. The communities they've built. Believe me—it's not a bad thing. Not at all."

"Why, Mr. Thomas," she says, leaning in, forehead to forehead, "is the big tough labor negotiator going all soft and domestic?"

"Well, no. Let's just say I want the same things that most men want. I want the little house and a little bit of security. That's all most laborers want, too. That's what I help them fight for."

She sighs. "But I don't have that kind of life here anymore, Jeb. I don't have the little house or the secure future. Not at all."

He tries to look sympathetic. "Okay. I understand that. But I'm telling you, if you go looking elsewhere, you're going to end up right back here. Not trying to discourage you. Just telling you a fact."

She plucks the grass from his mouth. "You're not discouraging me. It's my choice and I've made it." She kisses him quickly and replaces the grass.

He stammers for a moment, then sits up. "I suppose you know that properly escorted ladies would never kiss a man on just the third meeting."

"Thank goodness I'm a married woman who has already sacrificed her virtue." She looks him in the eye. "I'm a lost cause now, Mr. Thomas. Might as well just kiss a man if I enjoy him and have my fun."

Jeb turns his head and stares out at the long rolling lawn for several seconds. He likes this woman a lot. He likes her enough that he doesn't want things to move too fast. Yet she's the one who insisted they lay on the lawn beside each other, and she is the one who kissed him first. He tries to forget, for a moment, that he originally approached her for a far different reason—to find that blasted puzzle box—to follow a wild goose chase of possible riches.

Boxes and chases have been pushed to the background for now. He swallows and decides to take a chance. He says what he's thinking.

"You know, I haven't mentioned this before because I wasn't sure how to say it. But I'm not staying here long term. I'm on my way out by the end of the week. Eugene Debs is holding a big rally in Chicago, and I'm planning to attend."

Amanda nods. "I knew you were a traveling man when I met you."

"Then where does that leave us?" He looks back at her. "I mean … that kiss. This picnic. You're looking for more, and I think I want that, too. But this is my life right now. I move around. It's business, and I'll soon be on my way again."

"I'm not asking you to change. You are what you are. You do what you do."

"So I'll ask again. Where does all of this take us?"

"You said you're on your way out of Boston, Jeb. I … I guess I need to be on my way out, too. I think I need your help."

He looks at her strangely.

"No, I'm not asking you to take me with you. I know you can't, and it wouldn't be right anyway. I like to think I'm still a lady, in spite of all that's happened." She grabs his cap and pulls it over his eyes. "But I do want to know how you make your arrangements when you travel. How do you get by?"

"Ha. How? I get along by hook and by crook. Mostly I provide favors and wait for favors to be returned. People I've helped, they give me something back when they can. Free food. Free passage on trains, coaches, ships, whatever."

"And how will you get out of Boston?"

He smiles slyly. "I have railroad friends in most towns. That's all I'm going to say."

"You see? That's it. That's it exactly! People in the railroad business owe you favors. And I'm sure you can ask for a favor. Someone must know someone who hires maids and the like for private coaches. No? Those private railcars pull into the same stations as the rest of the train. Your friends have contacts there. Could you do that for me? Could you help me look?"

He laughs and tickles her nose with the grass blade before tossing it away. "Listen you, first of all, most of those rich folks already have maids that they must bring along on their trains. Second, if you're going to hang with me, you need to learn that I never actually come out and ask favors."

"No?" She looks disappointed.

"No. I do the favors for them first so that they owe me. It's all in how you approach things. I'd rather be owed than to owe."

She frowns and waits for him to explain.

He props himself up on his elbow again, clearly delighted to share his tricks of the trade. "Think of it like this. Say I wanted to get you a job on a train. Sure, I could go to all my friends at the station and in the rail yards. I could beg them for a favor. But where would that get me? I'd come off looking like a pest. Instead, what I do is talk to them about anything *but* a favor. And I slowly turn the conversation toward the problem of finding good help. Heck, my life is labor issues. People expect me to talk about workers." He leans forward, "But once we start down that road, they always talk about their own bad experiences. They talk about how hard it is to find good people. Eventually they rant about some job or another that needs to be filled, complaining all the while about the lazy people they've had working for them."

"Ahh. I think I understand. And you? You're the fixer?"

"Exactly. They tell me their troubles. They tell me who else is looking for workers and having trouble. That's when I offer to help." He smiles with satisfaction. "I sigh. I tell them it will be a stretch for me to assist them, but, hey … they're a friend. I can't just leave them in need. I tell them I'll *try* to help them."

She wags her finger at him. "So is that what you're going to tell me? That you'll just try to help me?"

"Well, I can't say that now. You know my trick. But that's essentially what I'll say to them. I'm sure I could go to the train station tonight, slink around, talk to some folks, and discover that this person or that person is looking to fill some slot. Any one of them can find some bum or hard-drinker to fill a job, but I can find them *good* people, and they know it."

"Don't your contacts worry that you'll send them some union troublemaker?"

"Oh, the person who actually does the hiring won't know that I'm the source. I work through my web of associates. I make sure they get the credit for finding the right person for the job. They love me for that. I feed them good people, talented people, and they are the ones who look like they have the great group of contacts. They shine as if they did all the work."

"Ahh."

"They actually do me a favor, but somehow I make them think I'm the one who has done a great favor for them. All in how you play it, hmm?"

Amanda dons a fake southern accent. "Why, Mr. Thomas, I do believe you are the most fascinating conspirator I've ever met."

He laughs and kisses her hand. The curve of her, as she lies on the ground, is fascinating, and he loses himself in that for a moment. And then for a few moments more.

Later in the afternoon, as they stroll back toward her temporary home, Amanda wonders if she should introduce

Jeb to the Morgans. The time may not be right. Just as she's mulling it over in her mind, they round the corner and spy the imposing house with Beverly and Jonathan standing on the front walk. They're talking to a policeman. Beverly holds a handkerchief. Her eyes are red. Jonathan points to an upper window. Amanda hurries up the walk, managing to catch the last of Jonathan's explanation.

"Came from right over there, I think. Right in the middle of the day. I don't believe the absolute brass of some people!"

With practiced formality, Beverly reaches out as Amanda arrives and takes her hand. "You don't want to go up into your room just yet, dear. It's a shambles."

Amanda frowns, looking at her, then at Jonathan. The policeman writes something in his book then walks a few feet away to look from a different angle.

"What do you mean?"

"We had a break-in," Jonathan says. "Broad daylight. I think he came across the rooftops of the other houses and must have climbed down into the attic dormer." He points up. "And right into your room."

"Oh ...."

Jonathan suddenly looks like he's in pain. "Oh, my rotten stomach," he says as he pulls a tiny bottle of Hostettler's Celebrated Stomach Bitters from his pocket and takes a long swig.

"That ain't going to help your stomach, sir," the policeman snorts. "That's stuff's nearly half alcohol!"

"I think that's actually the whole point of the silly product," Beverly says with dismay. She takes the bottle from her husband and puts it into her handbag.

Ignoring her, Jonathan points up to the roofline and continues his explanation. "Beverly heard something and went up to investigate. She surprised the burglar, who ran off. Might have been two of them. Thinks she heard another set of footsteps on the roof. Thank God they didn't attack her!"

Beverly shakes her head. "Yes, thank the Lord indeed. He was a sight, that man. Long hair. Puffy red eyes. A frightful-looking person. But he did bolt right back out the window when he saw me, thank goodness. But he was carrying some things when he fled, and I think they probably were your things, dear. He, or they, went back out the way they came in, across the rooftops."

Amanda's eyes widen. She turns and runs into the house, holding her dress up so that she can take the stairs two at a time. Second floor, third floor, then on up to the back attic. The others run behind her, with Jeb at the rear.

"Don't touch anything, dear!" Beverly calls out. "The policeman asked that we don't touch any ... Amanda? Please! Wait ...."

Amanda bursts into her room, brushing past another policeman, who tries halfheartedly to stop her. The place is indeed a mess. Dresser drawers are pulled out. The tiny closet door is open, and her clothes lay everywhere. She ignores all of it and drops to the floor, pulling herself half under the small bed. It's undignified, but she doesn't care.

She just pushes aside the shoes and clothes blocking her view. "No!" she gasps. "No, no. Please no!"

"What?" the policeman asks. "What's missing?"

"A box! My box!"

"You mean that silly puzzle box?" Jonathan asks. Both he and Beverley have ascended the stairs. They stand in the doorway surveying the mess.

"Yes. Yes!" Her voice is muffled, but there's obvious anguish in it as she pushes herself back out from under the bed. She crawls to the top of the bed, thrusting her hands under her pillow. She breathes a sigh of relief as her fingers find the diary. "At least he didn't get this. I never put it back in the box."

All eyes are on her as she sits on the bed, head resting on one hand as she grips the small diary tightly with the other.

A quick survey finds that the only other missing item is a five-dollar bill she had stored in a dresser drawer. Thankfully her other money, what little there was of it, had been deposited in a bank account at Jonathan's urging. Amanda reaches over to fluff her pillow, mainly to quietly feel if the silverware hidden inside is still there. Thankfully it is, and she keeps this information to herself.

Amanda, Beverly, and Jonathan all give statements to the police. Besides the missing money and puzzle box, there is also a broken window and a broken lamp.

Jeb has been standing quietly behind the whole group. Remembering her manners, Amanda finally introduces him to the Morgans, and Beverly regards him coolly. Eventually everyone files out of the house.

The policeman stops and looks back at her, as if remembering something. He jots a few words in his notebook, then continues down the front stairs.

Amanda bids Jeb adieu and returns to her room, picking up the scattered items from the floor. It takes only a couple minutes to drive home just how few things she actually owns. When she first left Wayne and the Cape, the lack of material things gave her a strange sense of freedom rather than a sense of loss. But as she stoops to pick up her meager dresses and books, she can only focus on all that she has lost, especially the silly puzzle box.

The tears come easily as she straightens the room, and she does nothing to hide them.

Chapter 2

Return

The first smell of land often arrives when a ship is still 100 miles from shore. Today, it wafts in on a western breeze, teasing noses and minds. On the land, wind moves over vegetation and across streams and lakes and raw earth, gathering an organic scent that then gets carried out to sea. It's the smell and the promise of things to come.

One whiff and a lonely sailor's stomach starts to ache. The longing builds.

Land sickness.

Victor Marius stands on deck of the French cargo ship *Porteur Sûr*. Nose to the air. Land is a welcome scent. After his shipwreck, after slowly coming back to his senses and not yet fully recovering from his wounds, the salty smell of the ocean tends to sicken him. How strange that seems. How could he ever dislike the water, which he previously had loved? But now he drinks in that distant smell of land, and longs for it.

His body is wracked with injury. Cuts and bruises on his shoulders, stomach, and legs make it hard to stand. His arm hurts. The bone is probably cracked. The vision in his left eye is out of focus. But he's here. He lives on.

He pulls on a squashed and discolored leather hat, one of the few items he still owns from before the shipwreck. It's always been in rough shape and it only survived because it was flattened and stashed in an oversized pocket of the clothes he wore on the day the ship went down.

Earlier in the day he found a short brass rod below decks. Now, as he stands topside, he lashes that rod to his forearm with two leather straps. He swings his arm a bit and can tell that the rod will help give him some extra strength and protection for the bone.

He also found an extremely heavy-duty leather vest in a heap of ropes. It seems older than the ship he's on and likely was once something worn by a French sailor during battle, to protect against flying debris. There are thin strips of metal sewn along the sides. With the vest laced tight, the cuts and bruises along his side seem less painful.

A deckhand approaches him and speaks in fractured, self-taught English. "No so long now, oui?"

"No. Not long at all." Victor gives him a grin. "Have you been to Boston before?"

"Once. Hope to see more this time. I look ... um ... how you say ... forward to it." The sailor asks his next question tentatively. "So I hear the talk that you – plucked from water days ago? Weeks maybe? Yes truth?"

Victor nods. "Yes. Truth, I guess."

"Bad luck, oui?"

"Oui. Bad luck indeed."

The sailor leans against the rail beside him. "What is this like for this to happen? I mean, all sailors, we think about that, oui? Maybe all who sail do such thinking? But who knows the truth of it? Only someone like you, no?"

Victor shrugs. "I guess I know what you're trying to ask. Other people have asked me the same question. It's very hard to answer." He looks at the sky, trying to find the right words. "It's like limbo. At least that's what it was like to me. At first you pray to be saved. Then you pray to die. But neither of those prayers is answered. Eventually I passed out. I thought I was done waiting. But I wasn't. I eventually awoke again and there I was still. The wait went on and on. I grew to hate the nothingness of that time."

The sailor nods. Victor can see the words do not give him any reassurance.

"Let me explain it another way. Eventually it was like drifting to sleep. I don't even remember being picked up. It's all like being lost in one big dream."

The sailor seems happier with this different answer. They talk a bit more, and then the Frenchman points to the horizon. As they debate how long it will be before Boston appears over the bow, two dolphins suddenly appear along the starboard side. Swimming faster than the ship, they dart back and forth in front. The two men watch the show for a while, and then the sailor excuses himself. Victor continues to watch the playful gray pair for several more minutes. It's a beautiful, peaceful sight. It's a sunny day and he's heading home. For the first time in weeks, he smiles. It's good to see these things: ships and Frenchmen and dolphins. It's good to feel the sun. It's good to be alive.

Chapter 3

Security

"What the hell do you mean it was the 'best opportunity'?"

Jeb should feel nervous challenging a man like Devlin Richards. Perpetual sneer and a knife in his boot, Devlin isn't a man to be trifled with. Yet Jeb doesn't care. He's angry. He's defiant. Maybe he's even a bit protective of Amanda, the nicest new friend he's made in many months.

"You heard me, Yankee. She was out with you for the day. It was a good time to move on it. That older couple, whatever their damn names are, we thought they were out, too. Didn't see a maid or anything. The timing was right, so we just went in."

Devlin tips backwards on the rear legs of his chair until he comes to rest against the side of a reddish-brown four-foot safe. It's one of several safes that line the small office at the back of Chen Lu's antique shop.

Chen Lu sticks his head through the curtain and presses a finger to his lips. Customers out front.

Jeb leans in toward Devlin, his voice only slightly lower than before. "So just who 'moved on it' as you say?"

"I did! All right? And Milton. He came with me."

Jeb grows furious. "What? You brought that pipe-sucking fool into her room? And you went through all her clothes, didn't you? Her drawers." He feels his hand clench into a fist.

25

"What do you care? Milton wanted to go. I needed a lookout. We did what we had to do. And you know it." He glares at Jeb. "We gave you those photos so that you could find the girl and tell us where she lived. You managed to track her down very quickly. Mission accomplished. So what the hell's the problem?"

Jeb shakes his head. "There are much more subtle ways to do it. I was getting close. She would have shown the box to me if I asked her to. She's been talking about moving away from the house, and I'm planning to help her with that. I would have had all the time in the world to get my hands on it and get it open. You didn't need to rush in."

"Well, now you don't have to worry about timing." Devlin nods toward the box, which is sitting in the middle of the table. "We got it, and Chen Lu will get it open. I imagine it will take him an hour. He probably won't want to break the box if he can help it. He's superstitious about that. Then we'll see what's inside."

Jeb nods. "Yes. We will. I'm going to stay right here at the shop until the box is opened. None of us seem to have much trust in the others, eh?"

Three long knocks shake the back door. His hand near his boot, Devlin shouts his okay and Milton stumbles in. After the door is closed and locked, Devlin relaxes and takes his hand away from his knife.

"What's going on?"

"Police out front," Milton whispers. "Coming in."

He looks hopefully at Devlin. A little information usually earns him a packet of white powder as reward. But Devlin waves him away.

Chen Lu peers through the curtain again. "Hide it," he says, finger waving at the box. "In the safe! Fast, fast."

The three look around the room, but it's Milton who springs into action. He snatches the box, pulls open the door of the big red safe, and slides it onto an empty shelf. Door closed, he spins the dial.

Devlin slips out the back, but Jeb decides to stay, not wanting to leave the box behind. He sits at the table, pushes the fidgeting Milton into the other chair, grabs a deck, and pretends they're playing cards.

The voices at the front of the shop are difficult to hear. Something about stolen merchandise. It's not clear how they made a connection back to Chen Lu's shop, but somehow they did. Jeb feels edgy.

Then he slowly realizes they're not talking about the stolen puzzle box. They're looking for other stolen items. Chen Lu has long been viewed with suspicion by the Boston police. Missing items have turned up in his shop before.

The police linger for so long that Jeb and Milton actually do start to play cards. It's a simple game of rummy, and they go through five hands before Chen Lu returns.

"Cops gone?" Jeb asks.

"Yes, but they return soon, I think. Not good. We need to find safer place for things, including new box." He walks to a large green safe and seems surprised to find it open and empty. "Where is box?"

Milton nods toward the red safe.

"What? In there? Why in there?"

"Isn't that the safe you always use?"

"No! I haven't used that one in over one year! Does not work!"

He tugs at the handle but the door doesn't budge. He spins the dial then slaps it in anger. "You fool! I can't get this open! Tumblers are cracked. What have you done?"

Milton looks down, then his face slowly forms into one of the most humble and idiotic smiles Jeb has ever seen. It's like he knows just what is coming and he accepts his fate. Chen Lu strikes the cowering man across the face, knocking him from his chair.

"Simpleton! Stupid bastard."

The shopkeeper reaches for a cane to continue the beating. Jeb stands and grabs it from the old man. "Stop it! We'll find a way to open it, okay? I know some mechanics down at the train yards. I'll get them to drill it out if we have to!"

Chen Lu pulls away. "I don't know how much time that could take. Very little time is what we have!"

"So I'll do it fast, all right? I have to go to the train station tonight anyway."

The old Chinaman sneers, but nods his agreement. Then he orders Milton to get out of his sight.

Chapter 4

Travels

That night in bed, Amanda slides the diary out from under her pillow and begins to read.

May 4, 1891

We've been in Cuba for several days, and at first I never felt happier. But that changed this morning. I received a cable just before noon that dashed my hopes for the long term.

I suppose it's a good thing that I'm not a drinking man, or I might have immediately bought a pint of cheap rum and drank my way right down to the bottom.

The telegram said that Westinghouse will not have the time nor the funding for me to pursue my experiments. They're very happy for me to continue my employment with them, but I'm to remain a manager of installations. Nothing more. Any engineering work I do will be done on my own, and the efforts should be directed toward solving problems that occur as a power system is built. As part of my job, I will continue to travel; I will continue to do all the same things I've been doing. As far as they are concerned, the status quo is just fine. No reassignment into research for me, and no special funding.

Blast it, when am I ever going to find the time and the funding to put my theories into practice? How can they be so shortsighted? Can't they see the wealth they could build from this new technology?

I immediately dashed off a letter to Tesla. I feel badly in need of his advice right now. He's been fighting this very same battle with Westinghouse, and I know he, too, is starting to pull free of George's control. Tesla says he may build a lab of his own in New York. I wonder if he'll actually have the nerve to make the leap. I don't know if he plans to hire anyone, but I would go to work for him in a moment if he needs me. Maybe I should visit him once I get back to the United States. Can you imagine? "Nikola? Hello! It's good to see you again. Say, could you give me a job? Let's invent something and change the world!"

I think he just might be interested.

I am convinced more than ever that radio is possible. I believe, if proven, that it will grow nearly as fast as the electrical power industry is growing. But the business aspect isn't the point right now. The real point is to prove that we have been right all along. I know it can be done, and I know we can gather the right people to do it.

I recently sent Tesla a sketch of something I hope to build. I think it's the solution to the distance problems we've been having for our broadcast tests. It's actually based on Nikola's new coil. We already know that we can create a signal, but as of right now, we can't sense that signal from any more than a few meters away. But I think I have the solution. I just need Nikola to help me work out the issues. Once we do, we can test the world's first radio broadcast over a distance. I know we can.

Amanda stops reading and looks toward her lamp. She's trying to understand just what it is that Victor wrote about with such passion. She thinks she understands the idea of radio from what she's previously read. A spark causes some sort of invisible wave, and other instruments can detect that wave. But what exactly is this good for? And the other terms scrawled on other pages—Tesla coil, amplitude—all of it seems very foreign. What she does find interesting is his passion for the whole business. She reads on, just to understand how it drives him.

Blast it again! Why is this company, with all of its riches and new business, so shortsighted about developing new technologies? My development costs would be minimal. At the most we'd need thirty thousand dollars to complete this experiment. But today's telegram confirms that our funding won't happen.

I have half a mind to take my research to Edison. Certainly he'd see the value in it! Surely he'd provide me with some funding! But I could never do that. Not after what Edison did to my friend Nikola. We'd both rather take this to our graves than to share it with that bastard Edison.

I took a walk down to the port-side shop today and visited my friend Mariana. I think it was to basically bid her good-bye. I have some decisions to make when I return to Boston. I have work to do and research to conduct.

I'm not going to stop working for Westinghouse because I can't afford to quit. But from this day forward, most of my energies are going to go into developing my own theories and setting my own path for the future. I'll go it alone.

I think I'll look up old Professor Alton when I get back home. He and I used to talk at length about radio theories. I think he might be pleasantly surprised at the progress I've made. Perhaps he can help me make it a reality. I'm sure he has no money for this either, but perhaps we could beg, borrow, or steal what we need from the Institute.

Unfortunately I'm supposed to be back in England by late June. We have another blasted installation to do. With Professor Alton's help, if he's willing to give it, maybe we'll be far enough along to do a long-range test by then. A month and a few weeks. Can we do it? If I can build a small tower to send the signal, and if I can figure out how to put some distance between myself and that tower, with nothing to block the signal, then I think I can finally do a proper test.

There's so much to do. And I need Tesla's feedback on my drawing. I also need to make the receiver smaller and more portable.

To hell with Westinghouse cutting my funding, and to hell with building a future with that company. I'm taking control of my own destiny. I'm going to make this work.

And then, as if to end his entry on an upbeat note, he scrawled in the margin. *Needed a hat while I was in the hot Cuba sun. Went looking for a straw boater but was only able to find an old top hat, leather rather than silk. It's a bit crushed at the top, which gives me a rakish look when I wear it. Kind of fun.*

Amanda sets the diary down on her chest and stares at the ceiling. The circle of light from her lantern dances like it's shining on water. Following its patterns gives her eyes something to do while her mind digests what she's read. The passage helps her understand a few more things about Mr. Victor Marius. He was quite a driven man. He didn't like to take no for an answer. She wonders how successful his experiments were. She wonders if he ever was able to conduct all the tests he wanted or if he was able to move his life in the direction that he had hoped.

She wonders what he must have looked like in that silly hat.

She also wonders how involved he became with his Cuban friend Mariana. Why did he decide to end it so abruptly?

And who is this Professor Alton? Is he someone she could find? Just a last name isn't much for her to go on.

She places a strip of ribbon in the diary to mark her place and then slides it back under her pillow. There is so much she would investigate if she had the time. But right now, she has other plans to make. Victor Marius and his explorations are interesting, but she has her own worlds to explore now. Her plans, when they fall into place, are not likely to include searching for a mysterious professor or learning what Victor was trying to do aboard a ship.

In fact, her interest in ships is waning for now. Her new mode of transportation, and for the time being, her new life, might just be the railroad.

Chapter 5

Connections

That evening, Jeb Thomas pays a visit to one of the six train stations that serve the city of Boston. He's hoping to chase down a supervisor, the one who directs the station's conductors and porters. The supervisor's name is Albert Jackson, and he usually has a sympathetic ear for the labor movement. Jeb forged an uneasy alliance with him during a previous visit over a year ago.

Entering through a side door, he finds Jackson sitting in his tiny office near the rear of the station.

Jackson manages to straddle two worlds. As the highest-ranking Negro at the company, Jackson sits in meetings with the white managers and owners. Articulate and intelligent, he is able to hold his own when they discuss work hours and the wages. The conductors and porters from this station are some of the best-paid union men around. Jeb knows that Jackson is the man to thank for that success.

It's actually rare to find Jackson in his office. He keeps his men on schedule by walking the platforms and weaving through the baggage rooms and rail yards. He chastises those who don't pull their weight.

Managers tend to view Jackson as just one of the workers. The workers tend to think of him as a manager because of his constant contact with the white bosses. It takes a man with strength, integrity, and a big chunk of self-esteem to walk the narrow path, keeping both sides appeased.

For that reason, Jeb's budding alliance with this supervisor is an uneasy one. Jeb senses that Jackson isn't quite sure what to make of him or his nearly religious faith in the power of unions. Men in Jackson's position sometimes treat unions as just another tool in their negotiations between workers and management. If the union gets too strong, or if management gets too strong, men like Jackson have less of a role to play.

A sign next to Jackson's door reads, "Boston Terminal Company." Jeb pokes his head inside and waves. This causes Jackson to laugh out loud, his deep bass voice shaking the room.

"Well, well, look who it is! Long time! Long time!"

They shake hands and Jackson invites Jeb to sit down. But first he asks him to shut the door.

"Did anyone see you come in, Mr. Thomas?"

"Please Albert, just call me Jeb."

"How about if I just call you a cab," he winks, "and that we get you out of here before my bosses see ya?"

"Just tell them that I'm not here on business. This is a social call. I'm in town and I haven't seen you in a quite a while. Just wanted to say hello."

Jackson pours some tea into a pair of tin mugs, setting the kettle back onto the hot edge of a corner woodstove. They chat and catch up for a bit. Jackson's kids are fine. The station is as busy as ever. Jeb's been traveling.

Then they elect to take a stroll outside, walking to the back of one of the empty platforms, away from prying ears and eyes. They pass a storage room that's overflowing, spilling its contents out onto the walkway. Jackson steers them around two large piles of baggage and some dirty mail sacks.

Jeb points to the mess.

"Oh that? Well, look at this place. You can't move in here anymore. We've done outgrown it. We needs a new station, and the owners are planning to build one. Problem is, this town has too many damn stations already. The politicians are delaying the plans."

Jeb doesn't understand. "What do you mean too many? If a city has a lot of rail stations, I'd say that's a sign of a strong economy."

"Well, you know what this building is, right? I work for the Boston and Albany Railroad Company. Yeah, you know all about that. Course, the New England Railroad Company, well, they've got their own train station too. And the Boston and Providence line, and the Old Colony Railroad Company—they've all gots their own stations and every one of 'em is so damn crowded with people and baggage that none of us can move. Just about every rail line is looking to expand right now because we keep growing."

"Yeah, and when business is growing, that's a good thing, right?"

"Hell yes," Jackson laughs. "I ain't saying it ain't good."

"So what does the name 'Boston Terminal Company' have to do with that? I saw the sign."

Jackson snorts. "Yeah, figures a man like you would want to know what that's all about. Eventually it's going to mean something to some of you labor boys, I suppose."

"Okay. Sounds like I need to know. So enlighten me."

"I ain't supposed to say much about it." Jackson smiles, enjoying that he can make Jeb wait for the info.

"But, hey, for a friend …," Jeb chides.

"Shit, Mr. Thomas, you still pretending to be my friend?" He laughs and kicks one of the mail sacks out of their way. "You don't think I see through that? I mean how often do I see you? When do I hear from you, hmm? I see you when you got business, that's when."

Jeb laughs. "Oh, come on. Who got you this job, Albert? Tell me that." Jeb is never quite sure what to make of a man like Albert Jackson. He's a new breed of Negro that America is only now learning how to accept. He's not content to lurk in the background, like so many other blacks in the years after the war. Nor is he brashly outspoken like old Frederick Douglass or current activists like Timothy Thomas Fortune. Instead, men like Albert Jackson are somewhere in the middle. Confident and straightforward. Not pretending to be white and not at all worried about being black. Not an activist. Not necessarily against activism. They just are what they are, and they conduct their business accordingly. It's a puzzling development.

Strangely, even though Jeb isn't sure what to make of Jackson, he's not particularly worried about him, either. He finds the man honest to a fault. The two of them – they know where they stand with each other, and that puts

Jackson miles ahead of many of the men with whom Jeb has to deal.

Jackson clears his throat and speaks in a mock-official voice. "My friends in the Order of Railway Conductors of America got me this job. That's who. Why? You going to tell me you had something to do with that?"

"Come on now, who is your union's best friend?"

"Damn, sir, you do like to collect your due, don't you?"

Jeb walks on with his hands thrust into his pockets. "No … no. You have it all wrong, my friend! I like to help! I'm in the business of helping!" Jeb points back toward the sign again.

Jackson slowly sips tea from the mug that he carries. "Well dang, I guess it won't hurt to tell you a little bit about it. I mean, if they hung that sign right out there in plain sight, they can't expect me to keep the secret, right?" He scratches his dark curly hair for a moment. "Okay, it's like this. The Boston & Albany here, they been looking to buy out the New England Railway. Least, that's what I hear from management. We been looking at the whole company mainly because we want to acquire the property where their old piece-of-shit terminal is sitting right now. You know, down by South Cove? Well, maybe you don't know all the terminals because you ain't from around here. But there's a big chunk of land behind that building. It would make a hell of a nice new terminal if we can get the whole piece. I hope we do. I could use a little more space my own self."

Jeb nods. It's not the kind of information he can turn to his advantage immediately, but it's certainly good to know.

"Trouble is," Jackson continues, "the city don't think our plan is a very good one. Boston already has so many train stations. We got tracks running everywhere, crossing streets, looping around buildings. It's a big old damn mess. City wants all of us train stations consolidated under one roof. One or two big train buildings, that's all they want. All the different lines would just meet up in one place. No one company would own the terminal building anymore. So they been blocking our efforts to buy the South Cove property, and now it looks like we ain't going to merge with anyone until the whole mess gets sorted out."

"Interesting."

"Yeah, ain't it though? I don't know if we should fight it or get on board with the idea. But the pressure's certainly on."

"Not just in Boston," Jeb tells him. "Other cities are already doing the same thing. Grand Central in New York. Union Station in St. Louis. Lots of cities are making the railroads merge their lines and running them into a single terminal. Sometimes the terminal's owned and managed by the city, sometimes by an association. But either way, there's lots of so-called 'union stations' being planned around the country. You can't fight it." Jeb shakes his head. "I have to tell you, though, as a union man, I hate to see the places called 'union stations.' Just doesn't seem appropriate."

Jackson shrugs with indifference. "Anyway, that's what the Boston Terminal Company is. It's just a name bolted to a wall right now. It's a couple of guys from each of the local railroads, and they meet in the office next to mine every few weeks. From what I've seen, mostly they just argue with each other. They only want the mayor to *think* they're working together."

"At least you get to keep an eye on them," Jeb kids. Then he tries to turn the conversation toward business. He tells Albert Jackson about a fledgling porters' union that's started in New York, but which seems to be gaining converts in the western and southern states, for reasons he can't yet understand.

"Why tell me about them? I got me a union already. You know that."

"Just thought you'd like to know. They need support. It's how things work. Unions merge with other unions. They grow stronger."

"Yeah, well, any of them show up here with a card, maybe I'll find work for them. That's all I can promise. We ain't going to join them directly."

"Yeah, I do know you always find work for my folks. That's what I like about this place."

Jackson tells Jeb his own tales of people coming to him constantly, looking for porter jobs, conductor jobs, even looking for work on the track crews, which is controlled by a totally separate and mostly white union.

Jeb nods. "So I guess that means you're already finding all the good people that you need, hmm? Without my help?"

"Hell no. Those that ain't drunk when they show up still don't have the skills they need. Seems that we fire almost half of what we hire."

Jeb points toward the longest platform. At the far end there's a group of private train cars parked on their own side track. Only a few of them have lights in their windows indicating that there are people inside. "Why don't you send some of your rejects down there to work? Maybe those rich bastards need some new workers, eh? You can keep your best men and send your dregs over there. Might be good for a laugh."

Jackson snickers. "Not a bad idea. I don't mine telling you, those private cars are a pain in my ass. Just one more thing to deal with."

They both sip their tea in quiet for a few moments. The evening is just cool enough that the hot tea makes their breath steam. A whistle blows off in the distance, and Jackson pulls a shiny brass watch from his pocket. Standard railroad issue with a bar across the top of the winding stem.

"The 10:28, right on time. She'll be here in a few minutes, and I'll have to go meet my men when it arrives." He looks toward the private car area. "Funny thing is, I would never send a bad worker their way, much fun as that might be. Them tips can be pretty good if you take care of such folks, you know what I'm saying?"

"I do. Yes."

"That means getting them fresh food, arguing with the track manager to make sure their little private car don't get stuck on some siding when they pull in. I baby them. I don't like them much at all, but I takes care of them just the same. Even make sure they find good help when they need it."

Jeb nods, finding his opening. "That makes sense. They're rich bastards, so they can pay."

Jackson laughs. "Hell yes."

"So who you sending them?"

"Well, right now, there's one family with two private cars that are always hitched in tandem. Two of them! Talk about money! It's like they have their own damn apartment building rolling around."

"Do their cars have a name? Some of them do. Lots of those rich folks like to name their cars, like they're passenger ships or something."

"Yes, they call it *The Duchess*. I'm not sure which of the two cars has that name. Maybe it's both of the fucking things together. But whatever it is, they've got more space than anyone needs if you ask me."

"Fine," Jeb says, "let them travel heavy. That's all the more help they'll need to hire."

"Oh, sure," Jackson snorts. "But they be fussy folk. I've sent three people to see them. They haven't hired a single one of them."

"No? Picky, hmm?"

Jackson just spits on the tracks.

"They must be bastards to work for if they're that picky. Maybe it's best that you don't send any of your good friends to them."

"Well, maybe. But like I says, I do like to take care of the rich folk if I can. Know what I mean? Hate that I haven't been able to do it this time. They're good to me when I deliver what they need. Bet they'll give me five dollars if I find 'em the right help."

Jeb pretends to think long and hard. "What are they looking for?"

"A cook. And a maid. Personal porter, too, I think, who would act more like a butler when they're underway ...."

"Where they headed?"

"Don't rightly know. Most of their trips are a week or two, then they're back."

The destination is one detail Jeb really wants to know. He wants to help Amanda, but he also wants to send her in a direction where he'll still be able to see her when he's able. Jackson is presenting a great opportunity, but it might not be the perfect match. Jeb isn't sure what to do.

He turns the conversation in another direction, asking about other jobs and other trains. He soon discovers that the private train car is the only real employment opportunity for a woman at this station, so he decides to try to make the connection.

"You know, Albert, I hate to see you miss an opportunity here. Maybe I can find someone for you. It's what I do, right? I may be able to come up with the right person for you to present to the owners of those train cars. Tell me what you're looking for."

"Oh, just someone reliable who doesn't look like a slob. Someone who can read. Someone with a good nature ...."

The conversation lasts until the 10:28 pulls in. Then Jackson excuses himself and hurries off. Before he goes, he talks bluntly to Jeb.

"You know how earlier you said that you don't know why the porters' union seems to be growing in the South and in the West?"

"Yeah. What about it?"

"I think I can tell you why. I had a cousin who's a railroad porter now. He's in his late forties. He couldn't find a damn lick of work in the South after the war. He ended up joining the Buffalo Soldiers, and he got his ass sent way out West. Did that for a few years then quit and became a cowboy—said he used to help drive the herds from Oklahoma all the way to Chicago."

"A Negro cowboy, eh?"

"Hell yeah. There's a lot more of 'em than you'd think. It's a tough life. Only tough and desperate men need apply. But it's not a bad life for someone who has few other options."

"But he got too old for cowboying after a while?"

"Not just that. Cowboy work's drying up. They don't drive the cattle much anymore. They put them cows on the trains instead. Cattle cars. So what's a cowboy to do? Sit around and piss and moan about having no work? Or does he go, cowboy hat in hand, to the very thing that stole his job?"

"I guess he goes right there. That what your cousin did?"

"Damn right he did. Porter work can be shit work, too. Hauling folks' bags. Always smiling and making nice and saying, 'Yes, sir. I's a good nigger, sir.' But it's steady and it's reliable. It's a warm place to sleep at night, and the trains ain't going away anytime soon."

Jackson turns to leave, his voice barely audible over the squeal of train brakes. "Anyways, I think that's why you see your porter unions growing in the South and the West. You've got your Negro ex-cowboys in the West and you've got your sons of ex-slaves in the South. They all need work and the trains turn out to be a good match for now. Porters and conductors and baggage handlers. You ain't going to see many white man at all in those porter jobs in a few years. You mark my words, Mr. Union Man. Negro men look out for each other, too, and they got the slots locked up. You want porter work? You talk to us. It's going to be our game. And after it becomes our game? Well, then no one else wants it. Then it's become 'black man's work,' and that's fine with me. More for us. That's the way it works, and you damn well know it 'cause you play the game, too."

With that, he walks up the platform.

"I'll see if I can send you someone for that maid's job!" Jeb calls after him.

Jeb heads home, trying to piece together his next steps, trying to figure out how he will cover up the fact that Amanda is a separated woman. He decides to try to pass her off as a single working woman who's had years of experience as a family maid. That might just work, if he can get her to play along.

Chapter 6

All That Remains

The *Porteur Sûr* sails into Boston Harbor, dropping its short sails, firing up its engines, and slowing to a crawl near Long Wharf. All the deep-water berths are occupied, and they end up having to anchor 200 yards offshore. So close, and yet so far.

Victor's passage back across the ocean was arranged by the ship's captain, who was amazed by Victor's story of survival. He wanted to do something to help, so Victor simply asked for his assistance in hitching a ride. Walking slowly up to the deck, he sees a tender is being prepared to take passengers to shore. He walks to the wheelhouse to thank the captain before leaving.

The day is gray, but generously warm. Back on US soil, he thinks for a moment about kissing the ground but doesn't want to make a scene. The customs process is almost nonexistent. Two men lazily scan incoming passengers to see if anyone looks dangerously ill. He walks through without a second glance and sets off on foot. After a couple blocks he opens his shirt collar and winds his way through Boston's spaghetti-tangle of narrow streets. He does not loosen the leather vest, grateful for the extra support it gives to his aching body. The walk slowly leads him away from the docks and into the city. Victor is home.

The only items he's owned for the past few weeks—a toothbrush, an extra shirt, and a light coat—were given to him by a pretty nurse back at the French hospital. They all fit into a small knapsack.

He's surprised to discover how weak he feels after walking barely a mile. His vision remains double when he's tired. He's not his old self yet, and it's frustrating.

He presses onward, stopping to rest every 400 yards or so. Walls, park benches — wherever he can sit for a few minutes. Thank goodness the brass rod strapped along his arm helps strengthen that part of his injuries. The reinforced vest helps, too.

Victor lacks the money to hail a taxi, so his initial destination is State Street and the tall thin office of the State Street Bank and Trust. A few weeks of pay should be waiting for him there, sent by Westinghouse when they learned he was alive and heading home.

Does he even still work for Westinghouse? It's not clear what his status is.

Does he want to still work there? The men in the suits had essentially shut down his experiments and told him to stick to electrical grids. Now that all the expensive equipment he borrowed is resting on the bottom of the ocean. They're likely very unhappy with him.

The money he's about to pick up may be little more than a severance check.

The teller behind the ornate brass grate is gracious enough, and in five minutes Victor is back out the door with a handful of bills. Hailing a hack, he slumps in the backseat, patting the coat pocket that holds his cash. He finally breathes a bit easier in spite of his sore lungs.

He gives some quick directions to the driver and collects his things as they pull up in front of his old lab. Because he's distracted, he doesn't see what the driver sees, but he does hear the man swear to himself as he pulls the horse to a stop.

"Jesus, mister, what happened here?"

"What do you mean?"

It's only then that Victor looks up to see the front of the building that once contained his lab. It's not at all what he left behind a few weeks before. The spaces that once held tall triple-hung windows are now dark, gaping holes. The second-floor windows are brighter, but that's only because the entire roof is missing and sun fills the space. There are black smoke stains above every opening, and the pungent smell of burned wood fills the air.

"Oh my God!"

Victor slides down from the cab and runs, as best he can, from window to window. The building is a total loss. Every inch of it is burned beyond recognition. It's a hollow black shell that will serve no future purpose other than as a target for a wrecking crew.

"No! Oh my God, I can't believe it! No!"

"You didn't know about this?" the driver calls out.

"No, I didn't! I've been away. I … I used to live here! And work here!"

The driver shakes his head. "Well, I'm sorry to hear that, sir. Least you wasn't inside when it happened." He immediately looks at his feet.

Up the street walks a brickie. Victor can tell he's a brick mason by the mortar splatter on his pants and the tools he carries.

"Excuse me, sir? Can you tell me when this building burned?"

"What, that one? Reckon it's been a few weeks now. Damn sight to see the night it burned, I'll tell ya. Flames must have been sixty feet high."

"Do they know what caused it?"

"Well, what I heard is it started in a workspace in the back. Owner kept a bunch of chemicals back there, they said. That's what caused it."

"What?"

"Yup. Landlord ain't happy with the renter, I hear. Blames him for it. Ain't been able to find the fellow, though. Kind of hard to hold someone responsible when you can't find him. Didn't find any bodies in the wreckage, though."

Victor nods slowly. "All right then. Th—thank you."

Victor tightens his leather vest and returns to the cab as the brickie walks on.

"Chemicals causing the fire?" Victor mutters to himself. "I don't think so. None of my chemicals would have caused that."

He walks down the side of the building and sees a pile of random items. They appear to be clothes, pieces of furniture and other things that were pulled from the building before the fire got too bad. Anything of value is long gone. He looks for several moments, then stoops to select just one item from the mound. It's his slightly squished leather top hat.

The driver just looks at him. Victor realizes he's waiting for directions. "Sorry. New plans … could you … um … could you take me to MIT? The college?"

The driver nods and they head back through Boston, toward Huntington Avenue and Copley Square. He needs a little help finding the campus, so Victor points out the correct turns. They eventually stop in front of a graying building on Garrison Street. A small sign in the front identifies this as the college's mechanical laboratories building.

As the cab pulls away, Victor looks at the front door for nearly a minute, trying to understand why he came. He finally decides it's because he doesn't know where else to go. With a deep breath and dirty hat in hand, he heads up the steps and checks a directory just inside the door.

Physics Department.

There he is. Professor Alton, Head of Mathematics and Analytic Mechanics. Second floor.

Chapter 7

Rooftops

The brass knocker on his front door bangs loudly. Jonathan Morgan, sitting in his front parlor, frowns as he looks up.

It's not the knock of a friendly neighbor. It means business. Jonathan tosses his magazine onto a table and walks out of the parlor, joining Beverly as she rushes up the hallway.

"Goodness," she huffs, "who in the world could that be?"

"I don't know. Let's have a look."

On the second floor, Amanda hears the knock, too, and quietly stands near the top of the stairs.

The middle panes on the front door are frosted green glass. Jonathan spies the top of a police hat before he opens the door. Then he sees two policemen, one behind the other.

"Is there an Amanda Malcolm living here?" the closest one asks.

"Malcolm? Well, we have an Amanda Grant who lives in one of our upstairs rooms. Why?"

The two policemen mutter to each other, and then the one in front says, "I think that may be her. Police business, sir. Could you ask her to come down?"

Beverly slips her hand around her husband's elbow and looks the front policeman in the eye. "Could you please tells us what this is about, officer?"

"She needs to answer a few questions. That's all."

"Well, that's more than a little outrageous," Jonathan remarks. "If you can't tell me what this is about, then I have no mind to let you in."

The officer shows him a piece of paper, then brushes past him into the foyer.

"Please! Please!" Beverly says. "Let me call her down." She walks to the bottom of the stairs and tilts her head back, looking up through the looping banister. She can see almost all the way up to the third floor. Amanda has already stepped back, pressing against the wall and edging quietly toward her room.

"Amanda?" she shouts. "Can you come down here for a moment? You have visitors!" Jonathan gives Beverly an angry look, like he was quite prepared to lie to the visitors.

Many windows are open throughout the house, and the draft coming up the stairs catches Amanda's bedroom door as she opens it. It swings wide, with a loud bang. The noise startles everyone and gives the police a reason to rush up the stairs. Amanda hears the footfalls and panics.

She's been worried about this very moment. It very well could be her problems back on the Cape have caught up to her. Wayne certainly did make threats. He could be very spiteful. She wondered if he might get the law after her, and now the law is running right up the stairs. She considers surrendering. She could just let the legal process sort things out. But how long would that take? They'd take her back to the Cape, back to Orleans, and Wayne has a long family history and many connections back there. He'd claim that she stabbed him. She ran away so she must be guilty, he'd tell the court. If things don't tilt in her favor, she could be looking at months, if not years, locked up.

She looks at the closet, then at the space beneath the bed. Could she successfully hide in either one? But she opts instead for the window since it's already open. Climbing out, she dreads that it might be too late, that there is nowhere to go on the Morgans' flat roof.

But then she remembers. The thief who took her puzzle box made it across the rooftops, didn't he? Despite wearing a dress and inappropriate shoes, she manages to rapidly claw and slip her way up the tin roof and onto the ridgeline of the row houses. Running down the length of two neighboring houses, she slides down the far side of one of the jagged peaks just as the police reach her window.

She can barely hear them, but she knows they suspect she's nearby.

"Out here? Did she go out here?"

Amanda strains to listen. Their words cut in and out as they move around, but she can pick out the basics of what they're saying.

"She must have. The window was open. Come on!"

"Hold it a minute," one of them demands. "Are you sure she was in her room? She might be hiding somewhere else upstairs!"

"Of course she was," Beverly says as she, too, steps out through the window, standing behind them on the roof.

"Now Bev, we don't know that for sure," Jonathan warns. "She very well could have gone out this morning."

"Nonsense, dear. I heard her moving about this morning, and we heard that door bang."

Jonathan bites his lip. "Could have been the wind, you know."

The police are unconvinced. One of them climbs up to the roof ridge, walking first one way, then the other. Amanda senses that the officer is coming closer, and she shrinks back behind a chimney. It blocks the policeman's view, and she uses that moment to run farther down the roofline. This last neighbor on the block has a hobbyist's coop on his roof set up for homing pigeons. Approaching it, Amanda considers crawling through the thick guano in order to hide inside. But then she sees that there is no real shelter in there.

Instead, she creeps toward the back edge of the house, crawling low to stay behind an eighteen-inch-high raised dormer. When she reaches the edge, she sees the wooden roof of a screened-in balcony. It's only about a foot down, but it doesn't make sense to continue out onto that balcony because it offers nowhere to hide. She sees a tree near the far end. Maybe she could leap onto its branches? She lowers herself slowly, trying to formulate a plan. It would be about a six-foot jump. It's risky, and if she misses the branches, it's at least a three-story drop to the ground. But if she does make it, she might be able to slide down the branches before they reach her.

As she slowly drops down onto the porch roof, one of the policemen reaches the final peak and starts to slide down onto the other roof where she was standing just moments before. The only reason he doesn't see her is that she's crouching low now, standing atop the covered porch and barely looking over the edge of the main roof. The sun is at her back. The policeman is squinting and trying to get his bearings.

It's only then that she sees the main roof overhangs the balcony roof by a short distance. There is a small space between the two. Amanda quickly lies down and rolls in, disappearing under the overhang like a sausage in a bun. It's a small, damp pocket, and it makes her shiver. The footsteps of the policeman vibrate the wood above her. Did he see her? Or is he looking toward the tree, thinking she might have gone there?

She closes her eyes and waits, barely breathing. If he jumps to the balcony to look over, he may see her. But he doesn't move. After a half minute, he walks on. The sound of his footsteps comes and goes for the next ten minutes, then she hears him clunk back up the roofline toward the Morgans' house.

"I don't know if she came up here or not," the policeman shouts to his associate. "But she's certainly not here now."

"She has to be!" Beverly insists.

"That's not so at all, Beverly!" Jonathan interjects, his anger mounting.

"Go look for yourself," the policeman says to Beverly. "Nothing to see over there."

Amanda listens to the voices fade. She's afraid to move and stays put for nearly an hour.

Back inside the Morgans' home, Jonathan demands that the police tell him what all the fuss is about.

"Tell me, how well do you know this woman?" one of the officers asks.

"Well, we didn't know her at all until she came to us for help a couple weeks ago."

"Help?"

Beverly crosses her arms. Jonathan tries to sound supportive and caring. "Sent here by a friend. She was moving back to Boston after living on Cape Cod for a while. She was leaving her husband, apparently."

"Well, the friend who sent this woman your way may not have known it, but Amanda Malcolm, now apparently calling herself Amanda Grant, is wanted for attempted murder."

"What?" Beverly gasps. Her hands press to her breast.

"Attempted murder? Attempted on whom?" Jonathan challenges.

"Apparently she tried to stab her husband."

"Oh, balderdash. I was told that he was known to hit her. She probably just got tired of it and hit him back. Doesn't seem like a major mystery, does it?"

One of the policeman shrugs. The other emits a short chuckle.

They continue to talk as they wind their way back down the stairs, eventually reaching the front door. Out on the portico, one of the policemen writes something in his book. "Look, sir, all I know is her husband made a claim and someone considered it serious enough that the problem has followed her all the way up here. It's not up to me to decide whether it's legitimate or not. The courts will have their say. I just need to pick her up."

He delivers his next words with careful precision. "At this point, it doesn't appear that you had any knowledge of her past. But keep in mind that harboring a fugitive is a serious charge. Now that you know what's going on, you have a responsibility to turn her in if you can. Understand?"

Jonathan snorts. Beverly says they're happy to cooperate.

The policeman flips back a few pages in his book. "Also, before I came here, I looked in the records. Your house was broken into recently, correct?"

Jonathan nods.

"Well, that helped us put two and two together—when she reported the box stolen and gave her name. One of our men came back to the station and looked up that name. He made the connection by also looking up her maiden name through the marriage records. Smart man, that one. He's going to be a good cop."

"I see."

"You tell us if she comes back, you hear?"

The policeman hands him a small card, then the two officers head back toward their precinct house.

"Well, I never," Beverly stammers as Jonathan closes the door.

"I know it. That poor dear. Can you believe the nerve of her husband?"

"What?" Beverly looks shocked. "I wasn't talking about her husband. I meant that I can't believe all the serious problems this girl has. She's a criminal! And she's brought the crimes right into our house. She can't stay here one more minute, Jonathan!"

"Beverly, please, can't you see what's happening here? It's not her. It's her husb—"

"I'll have none of that, Jon," she interrupts. "The police have never, ever visited us before. Yet they've been here twice since she arrived. Who knows what they were really looking for in her room? Were they just looking for her? Or were they looking for something else? Maybe she steals. Maybe she's involved in that terrible opium. Who really knows?"

"Oh Beverly, Beverly. You're unbelievable. Look, I'll talk with her."

"No. You'll evict her, dear, and you'll have the police waiting for her when you do!"

"I will do no such thing."

They exchange bitter glances. Jonathon slowly acquiesces.

"Well, I won't have the police here, anyway. But I will ask her to leave. I can understand that much, and I suppose it's time."

"See that you do." Beverly walks briskly away, her bustle swaying behind her like a pendulum.

Chapter 8

Lady

Amanda emerges from her hiding place, stealthily making her way back across the rooftops and into the Morgans' house. She waits until Jonathon and Beverly spar in disagreement on their back porch then uses that time to move quietly down the stairs and out the front door. She makes her way to Jeb's rooming house, nearly crying, full of anger and spouting an urgent tale of a husband chasing her down, the Morgans throwing her out, and, for God's sake, why don't things ever go as planned, and ... and ....

He gives her a hug and two hankies. Both soon grow wet with her tears. She frets and twists them in her hands like the wrung necks of miniature swans.

Jeb agrees to return with her to the Morgans' to help her pack her bags. Silence hangs like a lead cloud as they knock on the door. Jonathan allows them to come in. Beverly's watchful eye evaluates their every move as they ascend the stairs and gather Amanda's belongings.

The only sound is the squeak of the closet door and the rustle of clothing as it's folded. Jonathan, his voice carrying a tone of sad resignation, promises not to call the police. As Jeb and Amanda leave the house, Beverly doesn't respond to Amanda's thank you.

"So what do you think?" Jeb tries to lighten the mood as he totes Amanda's bags. "That woman was looking at me like I'm a charlatan. Thinking that I must be taking advantage of you, maybe? Or maybe she was thinking that she should actually warn me about getting involved with the likes of you?"

Amanda looks hurt at first, then manages a meager laugh. By the time they return to the rooming house, she's in slightly better spirits.

But the change in her standard of living is immediately apparent. With little money between them, she and Jeb cook pork fat on the house's shared woodstove, and they eat on the back porch. Before nightfall, Jeb collects chair cushions from around the house and uses them to make himself a bed on the floor of his room.

"Don't be silly," Amanda whispers. "Let me sleep there. I can't put you out of your own bed!"

But he insists, and they settle in, bidding their good nights. Their sleep is a restless one. This very act of closeness, sharing a room though not yet a bed, changes something between them. It draws them closer. She knows Jeb has wanted this change, but he has proceeded ever-so cautiously.

He continues to treat her like a lady. Yet they both know a proper lady would never stay overnight un-chaperoned at a man's house, and she would certainly not sleep near him. It was too close. Too familiar.

Likewise, a proper gentleman would never allow it. And a proper gentleman should have much more to offer a woman than this.

That is the essence of what has changed between them. He isn't really a gentleman. For now, she is just fine with that. That also means she isn't much of a lady anymore. They are simply doing what they have to do.

She might actually enjoy not being a lady.

Amanda stares at the rooming house's dark ceiling. *Maybe Beverly was right. Maybe I am spiraling down into some kind of Bohemian trash. I tried to live the right kind of life, didn't I? But I'm right back here in the dirty part of the city. Lost. Marginalized. Maybe this is where I belong.*

There is a strange comfort in this. There's a certain freedom in a hand-to-mouth, always-on-the-move lifestyle. If social mores no longer apply to her, then she's completely free to enjoy a much different kind of life.

But she still hasn't reached the point where she'd take a man who is not her husband into her bed. Perhaps it's just not the right time, nor the right stage of this big adventure.

Chapter 9

Borrowers

The man seated behind the desk in the MIT classroom is dressed exactly the way Victor remembers him. Gray suit, worn at the elbows. Out-of-date tie. He even wears, with charming obliviousness, a pair of scuffed brown shoes.

Gold wire-framed glasses sit close to the end of the professor's nose.

Only the hair is different. As unruly as ever, it's now gray throughout instead of just at the temples. The old man, hunched over a large book, is lost in thought. He doesn't notice that someone else has entered the room.

Victor clears his throat. "Excuse me. Sir? Professor Alton?"

The man at the desk blinks as if awakened from a dream. When he looks up, there is no immediate recognition in his eyes.

"It's Victor, sir. Victor Marius. A former student of yours."

The professor takes off his glasses, cleaning them. "Oh? Well, hello … yes, welcome back. … So, what year did you attend …?"

Then a flash of recognition reaches the professor's eyes. His glasses drop to the desktop.

"Oh my! Yes, of course! Victor! Oh my goodness, how are you, my lad?"

They meet in the middle of the room, embracing more as friends than as teacher and student. Professor Alton gestures to the chairs in the front row. "Sit, sit, sit! Please! It's been so long. Do forgive an old man for not recognizing you at once. It's so very good to see you!"

Victor thanks him. "It's good to see you, too, professor!"

"Now let's see," Alton tries to remember. "After you left here, you went to work for a firm right here in town, didn't you?"

"Yes, sir. For a few months. Then I headed to Pennsylvania for a bit. I guess that's when we lost contact."

"Of course! You went to Westinghouse! I remember your letter. We were all very proud of you here, Victor. Expected great things from you. Still do! But you're correct. We all did lose track of you after that. What has it been now, six years?"

"At least that, or more, I'll wager."

The professor nods. "Time flies so quickly, doesn't it?" He gives a paternal smile. "You were always one of my brightest students, Victor. Yes indeed, definitely one of the good ones."

Then the old man laughs suddenly, recalling some past event. "Well, let's say you were one of the hardest working. What you occasionally lacked in common sense, you more than made up for in hard work."

Victor chuckles. "You're too kind, sir. So tell me, did they ever replace your desk?"

"That's the replacement right over there!" The professor looks around the room, then leans close. "Exactly how you managed to set it on fire, I'll never know."

"I'm not entirely sure myself, Professor, but I learned a lot that day about why wires should be insulated."

With a flourish they exchange a few more stories, and Alton tells Victor bits and pieces of news about his old classmates. Several of them, it seems, also ended up working in the electrical or telephone industries.

"No one else has been interested in radio waves though. Isn't that the interest you developed in Pittsburgh?"

"Yes, sir. I guess you do remember the details of my letter from some time ago. Though it was an extremely vague concept at that time."

"Indeed I do. I gave it some thought." He leans forward, his voice dropping like he's whispering to a spy. "So tell me. Those ideas you had. The devices and such. Did you ever pursue them?"

Victor nods. "Indeed I did, sir."

"Yes, yes. I thought as much. One can't keep you away from things once you think an idea is a good one. You know, I almost failed you your last semester because you spent so much time working on electrical transmission experiments instead of on your official studies. Couldn't do it, though. You were a smart lad, and you deserved to graduate."

Victor laughs. "Oh? Is that why you'd visit me in the lab every other day? To pull me away from my tests because I wasn't studying enough?"

Professor Alton waves the comment away.

"As I recall," Victor continues, "you actually used to look over my shoulder and make some very valuable suggestions on how to proceed."

Alton laughs hard, until the laugh dissolves into a deep cough. "Like I said, you deserved to graduate, mainly because I knew you didn't have a teacher who made you stick to your proper studies. I always let you run a bit wild with your ideas, didn't I?"

Victor nods. "I had a teacher who inspired me. That's more important."

Alton shrugs. "Well, a professor can spend only so much time on theory. I don't get to see the practical application of scientific research nearly as much as I'd like. We do the research here. Someone else gets to make the ideas a reality. It's not fair for a man like me. So it certainly was exciting for me to see you trying to do both."

They both laugh now, lost in a shared memory.

"Damn near killed yourself with a shock once, lad. Remember that?"

"Oh Lord, yes. How could I forget?" Victor holds up his left hand. "See this fingernail? It never has grown straight since then."

Alton wipes his eye. "Enough reminiscing! Just tell me what happened at Westinghouse! Did things work out well for you there?"

Victor tells his story, including his various attempts at radio research. The fight for funding. The small projects with borrowed equipment and makeshift lab space. The late nights and the slow progress.

"There really is such a thing as radio waves reaching over a distance, sir. We were able to prove that much at least. In the lab. Others have, too, though none of us know yet how far they can reach."

The old man's eyes widen. "Yes, yes, I knew it! You must share your notes with me if you can."

"But I haven't any notes left. That's one of the reasons I'm here. My lab is gone." He tells the professor how he just discovered that his lab was destroyed by fire.

"Terrible, terrible luck, Victor. I'm glad you came to see me, but I don't know what I can do. I wish there was something."

Victor doesn't want pity. Instead he wants to tell the professor more about what he's discovered. "We created a signal. From a simple spark. We received it right there in the room. At least it seemed like we did. We did it more than once and kept increasing the distance. We needed to get farther away to make sure the signal really travels the way we think it does."

"And did you?"

"Well, I tried. But things didn't work out." He tells Alton the story of his other work at Westinghouse—of his travels to help install lighting systems, and his former love of the sea. He tells of how it seemed natural to use a ship. Ships were docked right down the street when he wanted to test his radio idea across a much wider space, and how all was lost—on what should have been a simple voyage.

The professor listens with sympathy. "Thank goodness you survived, Victor! My, what an experience. And what about your equipment?"

"All lost, too, sir. One of a kind. I could rebuild it, I suppose. But I had to scrounge so very hard just to gather what I used the first time. I don't think I could go through all that again."

The old man nods. "Your luck is even worse than I realized, Victor. I'm truly sorry. But surely the folks you work for are impressed enough with what you've done to let you continue."

"They make no money at all from my radio research, Professor. They really just want to sell generators, lights, converters. That's their main business. What I'm doing is too expensive, and too tentative until it's proven. They really have no idea how much money could be made from radio. In fact, neither do I."

Alton thinks for a moment. "That madman Tesla works at Westinghouse, doesn't he? I'm sure you must have met him."

"He does, sir. And I did meet him. He became my mentor there. And I certainly don't think he's a madman."

"No? I met him at a conference once. Had some great ideas about moving alternating electrical current over great distances. Had some ideas about the possibility of radio waves too. At least we agreed on that much. But then our conversation veered off on some side trip that had me totally confounded, Victor." The professor squints, recalling the talk. "Tesla said something about blasting out electrical signals that could reach all the way around the globe. Not radio like you're testing, but actual electricity, traveling through the air. Ramblings about wires carrying pictures. Global signals carrying voice, moving images, everything. The man is either insane, or he's letting his dreams get away from him. He doesn't seem to want to remember the true physical realities of the world."

Victor smiles. "He is indeed eccentric, sir. I'll agree with that. But some of his ideas do have merit."

"Well, if you say so, my boy. Personally, I'd rather read a Jules Vern story. They're just about as believable as some of the stuff I heard Tesla spout, and I daresay Vern seems to have a better grasp of physics."

Victor feels the urge to defend his friend, but he can't hide his amusement at the comment.

"But seriously, Victor, what brings you here? Are you looking for help?"

"I don't know, Professor. I guess I just didn't know where else to go."

"Why, you go back to Westinghouse, of course! It's a growing company! They need ambitious young men like you! And you certainly seem to want to get back to work."

Victor shrugs. "I don't know how ambitious I feel anymore. I still feel half dead from my ordeal."

"Nonsense. You look strong enough. You look no worse than a man getting over a good bout of the flu. Just give it a few more weeks, my boy."

"Kind of you to say, sir." Then he leans forward, chin on his fingertips. "Truth is, I'm not sure if Westinghouse will have me back. I wasn't exactly the easiest employee to supervise."

"You, Victor?" Alton says with a wink. "I can't imagine."

"The problem is, I as much as told them I was going to make time to do my radio experiments, and that they would just have to accept that. I was supposed to go to San Francisco to supervise a generator installation, but I insisted on coming back to Boston with my equipment and taking my boat trip. I told them I'd be gone for a couple weeks, and it wouldn't be a big deal since they hadn't yet shipped the generators to San Francisco. That certainly didn't make my immediate supervisor happy. In fact, when Tesla wrote a note on my behalf, it just made him mad."

Victor shakes his head, recalling how the whole thing played out. "If I had been successful with the tests out there on the ocean, I'm sure everything would have been forgiven. I'd have proven something important, and maybe the company could have made a little money from my discovery. But, as you know, that didn't happen. So now? Well, now I have nothing. I took a gamble, and it didn't pay off. I basically made my supervisor angry. I disappeared for weeks, leaving him in a lurch. I chased a dream that no one else believed in, and I turned out to be a fool. On top of delaying everything else, I also lost over a thousand dollars' worth of the company's equipment when the ship went down. It was my only working prototype."

Alton nods slowly. "So you're telling me that essentially you haven't changed much since you were here. You're still losing stuff and wrecking things."

Victor laughs. "No sir, I guess I haven't changed much at all."

The professor walks to his desk to retrieve a notebook. "Let me send a few telegraphs on your behalf, son. I'm not sure if I can help, but I do know a few local people in your line of work."

"Thank you, sir. I appreciate that." He pauses for a moment. "I … I guess the bigger question, though, is where this leaves our work."

"*Our* work?"

"Yes, sir. You know what I mean. A lot of my theories are based on things I learned from you. Not in the classroom, but in the lab. You know of which I speak."

The old man looks out the window. "I have no work. Just ramblings of a foolish dreamer. You know that."

"Seemed like more than that to me, sir. I found it inspiring."

The professor shakes his head. "When we get to talking about such things around here, the theories versus the realities, I like to compare it to a bunch of drunks arguing about religion or politics. Things start out interesting, but the thoughts, especially when it comes to theories like radio, amount to nothing logical. When I told you some of my preliminary ideas, it was mostly gibberish. No more. No less."

He gives Victor a serious look. "How much—if anything—that I told you about the idea of radio ever made it into your real-world tests?"

"I don't know. Maybe 10 percent. But the important thing is that those ideas provided inspiration for all of it, sir. Maybe Tesla couldn't make things happen exactly the way he wanted, and maybe you couldn't either. But when I listened to both of you, I connected the dots. I took the best ideas from both, and I made it actually happen, sir! We made a radio signal, and I think that it really can be sent the way we need it to be sent!"

"If you did, then I'm proud of you. But so what? Even alchemists seem to have microscopic, barely measurable successes now and then. That doesn't mean what they are chasing is real. It doesn't mean it can be scaled to anything that works economically."

Victor stands, running his fingers through his hair. He looks like he wants to pull a handful out by the roots. "Damn it, Professor, is that really what you think? That what we talked about can never be made real?"

Alton sighs, and to Victor the man suddenly looks very old. "A lifetime of failure can take its toll, Victor. I've banged my head on the same wall for years. The difference is I've found my success in other ways. As a family man. As a respected professor. I'll retire soon. Did you know they plan to name a chair for me? The Alton Physics Professorship. It makes a man proud. If I had spent my life chasing fiction and fantasy, I don't think that level of success and recognition would ever have happened."

"You're the one who convinced me it *could* happen, sir."

Alton looks out the window. "I know I did, lad. And I wonder now if I did a disservice to you by doing so. Look at you. Almost thirty. No family. Everything lost. You might not even have a job anymore. When I look at you, I see myself, Victor. I see what I could have become if I had chased my obsession as hard as I wanted to when I was younger."

He places a hand on Victor's shoulder, his voice just a whisper. "You want to see what obsession and passion does? Just look at your other mentor. Does Tesla seem normal to you? Could he ever be a professor at a place like this? I don't think so. Could he ever be pulled out of his lab to lead a company like Westinghouse? No, I think not. He's passionate, but far too consumed. Do you think old George will even keep him around long-term? Once they build their huge systems, that will be that. Don't end up like Tesla, Victor. Those crazy 'Tesla coils' of his, and the sparks they make while they do nothing. Good God!"

"You know about those?"

"Oh, yes. He hasn't published any papers yet, nor publicly displayed them. But we've all heard about the concept and seen some photos. He's going to kill someone someday."

"What makes you think he hasn't already?"

They look at each other for a long moment.

"And you'd go back to all that if you could, Victor?"

"In an instant."

"You're a foolish young man, Victor. But some part of me does admire your passion." He prepares to leave, gathering some papers from his desk. "Unfortunately, I have a meeting in another building in a few minutes. But I certainly would like to continue this conversation. Perhaps dinner this evening?"

"I'd like that, sir."

"Where are you staying?"

"Nowhere, yet. I haven't even planned for that."

"Hmm … well, I wish I could offer you lodging, but I recently moved myself. Sold my home. I rent a room now, not far from here."

"That's all right. Don't worry about it."

"Can I give you money to rent a room of your own for a week or so?"

"No, sir. Thank you kindly, but I don't need that."

The professor nods. "All right, then. Just dinner. Let's plan on it. And I will make some inquiries on your behalf. You have too good a mind to let it sit idle, Victor. The least I can do is to help you put it to work."

Victor shakes his professor's hand. "I do appreciate that, sir." He starts to leave, then turns back. "Your ideas were not fantasy, sir. They were valid. I may not yet know what their practical application might be. But I did want you to know that you were on the right track."

The old man nods, but says nothing.

After they part company, Alton takes a long roundabout walk to his meeting, staring down, staring at sidewalk cracks, then at floor tiles as he enters a lobby. He sees none of them. In his head he sees formulas, and the hazy images of strange equipment. He sees the warm comfort of his office, family, and classroom. He has no regrets for making his choices. But there are other pictures in his mind, too. The opportunities missed, the roads not taken.

Perhaps he's a foolish old man who took the easier path. If that's true, he would find some kind of redemption in helping Victor. If Victor's experiments really do work, it would make him proud.

Yes … he could help. It's just a matter of scouring the Institute and borrowing the right equipment.

He also noticed that Victor's eye isn't quite right. Perhaps a result of his ordeal. Well, he has lenses of various sorts. He could also build something for Victor, if he's willing to wear it.

Chapter 10

Alexanders

The next morning, Jeb and Amanda enter the railroad station just before 9:00 a.m.

Safety is always a problem for a labor organizer. Jeb looks around, worried that the railroad guards and yard foremen, "bulls," as the transients call them, may be on the lookout for him. Railway owners don't take kindly to a union organizer talking to their workers. Jeb has been escorted out of railroad buildings more than once—the last time with a fist driven so hard into his stomach that he spent a half hour throwing up in a gutter.

"Feel safe?" Amanda whispers.

"Yes," he says, with only a little hesitation. "A lot of the men in this building seem to like me, for which I'm grateful. I think we're okay here in broad daylight. As least for now."

He can always tell the men who appreciate his work. They're the ones who believe they're getting a rotten deal. The ones who have worked far too hard for far too long and who want someone, anyone, to reward their sore backs and hardscrabble lives. These are the men upon which Jeb always focuses. The ones he wants to meet, console, and organize. Get the disgruntled and vocal minority on board in any city, including Boston, and others usually will follow.

Friends also help him escape. When his cause is their cause, they find ways to give him a free ride. One time via a lumpy sack hidden in a dark mail car.

In good times, and there have been a few good times lately, some conductor would unlock an empty compartment in a first-class car. There he would sit quietly and travel in style, sleeping well, stretching out in comfort and smoking the free cigars that had been left for him. His travels were luxury or hardship, with little in between.

Jeb doesn't know what to expect today. And he feels unsure of where things stand with Albert Jackson.

Jeb finds a place for Amanda to sit in the station's lobby.

"But what about the policemen?" she asks. "Won't they find me?"

"You think any cop walking the beat around this station even knows what you look like? They don't. You'll be fine."

He grabs an old newspaper off one of the benches. "Here. Read this. Cover your face. You'll get by."

With Amanda occupied, Jeb walks to Jackson's office, carrying Amanda's bags with him. Finding the office empty, he takes a deep breath and sits behind the desk, willing himself to take on a smug attitude. When the conductor returns from his rounds, he finds Jeb with his feet up and a big smile on his face.

"What the hell are you doing?"

"I'm here to give you a Christmas present, my good man. Christmas in July!"

"What the Christ are you talking about? Did anyone see you come in here?" He looks down the hallway. "You need to leave."

"Relax, Albert. Are you ready to receive a big tip from the owners of that private train car? The fancy Alexander rig parked out there?"

"Oh Jesus. Don't tell me that you—"

"That a problem? I told you I'd find you a maid for them. I thought you'd be happy!"

The conductor looks down at the bags. He can tell that they're a woman's bags. "Well, I might have been happy, but not like this. They've got to meet her first! I've got to know who I'm referring. But it looks like you've got her all ready to move in!"

"I know, I know. Merely a formality. Believe me—she's that good. They won't say no to her."

"Where is she?"

"Out in the lobby. If you want to meet her, let's go."

Jackson looks at the luggage again. "This is a load of horseshit, isn't it? I know how you operate. If you're moving this fast, it's for a reason."

Jeb reaches for Jackson's cigar box. "Don't know what you're talking about."

Jackson steps forward and snatches the box away. "Don't give me your shit. You're not doing me any favors. You're playing one of us off the other, ain't you? Got some promise to her, just like you got some promise to me, and you're trying to make both sides think it's some kind of damn 'favor'."

"Nope. Definitely don't know what you're talking about, Albert."

"Well, I do. You got yourself a little ahead of things this time. And now you come here, needing me to act real quick-like just to bail you out."

Jeb shrugs. "Look, you don't have to do me any favors, Albert. But, yes, this girl lost her place to stay, and I figured if I could get her this job quickly, then she won't have to worry about where to stay for a few days. I figured if you liked her, she could move right into the job and she wouldn't have to pay for a room. That's all."

"Jesus." Jackson shakes his head. "I should say the hell with you and the hell with your plan."

"You could. But then this may pan out exactly the way it needs to, and you'll end up doing a favor for some rich folks. Make sense?"

Albert Jackson says nothing.

"Well, why not at least come and meet her? If you decide to call everything off after that, fine. However, I think you'll be impressed and happy to introduce her to the owners of that Alexander car. It ain't going to cost you a nickel, and it might get you a nice cash tip."

Jackson grumbles, then agrees to take a look. But he refuses to walk through the station with a union representative. Jeb goes out to the lobby first. He leans against a far wall. As Jackson approaches Amanda, the man's eyes brighten considerably. He obviously wasn't expecting someone like her.

Amanda looks surprised when he stops to talk. After a few moments, he nods toward Jeb, mouthing the words. "Okay, fine."

This just might work after all, Jeb thinks to himself.

The three of them reunite in Jackson's office, door closed and shade drawn.

"If we do this, you owe me one union man, you hear? I don't owe you."

"I hear, I hear," Jeb acknowledges.

Jackson heads toward the back of the station. leaving Jeb and Amanda alone in his office. Jeb slumps into the desk chair. "That's what I try to avoid, you know?" he says. "Having people say, 'You owe me one,' but at least we've got a shot now."

She smiles at him. "I appreciate all you're doing for me. I really do."

By the time Jackson returns, there are a couple policemen lingering at the far end of the hall. Jeb pulls his hat low, and Amanda looks away as they quickly head toward the back of the station. They emerge onto a rear part of the train platform that's closed to the public. There, decoupled from the regular passenger trains, sit a series of private railcars. These cars drip luxury. Most are custom rigs built by companies like Jackson and Sharp or Pullman. Amanda's eyes widen as she looks through one of the windows. Marble-top tables support ornate brass lamps and silver trays. Larger tables are trimmed in fine linen and hold crystal stemware. Tiny clips stick up through the tablecloths. These pinch the bottoms of stemware glasses, holding them in place during travel. She understands instantly why the owners of these cars desire their own servants. The cars serve as full houses on wheels. A full staff is needed just to keep them in operation.

"Mrs. Evans will be here shortly," says Jackson. "She'll probably ask a lot of questions, but I've found her to be a pretty nice lady. Just smile and nod, and she'll think you're very pleasant. Think you can do that?"

Amanda smiles and nods, just to show that she can. Jackson chuckles.

Jeb lets out a low whistle when they stop at the Evans' cars. "Look at this rig. These people have some money, or what?"

Jackson strokes the metal sides of the car. "See here? This is the main parlor car. The family sleeps in a separate car behind."

Jeb stoops to look under both cars, studying the wheels and suspension. "Neither of these coaches are more than five years old," he guesses. "But you said they just finished remodeling them?"

"Yup. Guess they weren't near fancy enough. All new paneling inside now. Furniture, dishes, the works. This will be its first time out since they upgraded 'em. That's why they're looking for a new crew. These rigs apparently haven't been used in over a year."

Above the door, the words "The Duchess" are painted in blue with gold highlights.

"So what does this Mr. Evans do for a living?"

"I understand he owns a textile mill up in Lowell. Second-generation owner. Money to burn."

"All on the backs of underpaid workers," Jeb sneers. "Bet we could organize a strike up there just by dragging this car to the front of the factory. Show them how their boss likes to spend his money!"

Amanda grabs his arm. "Stop it, Jeb. I'm just happy to be considered for this job. Let's not complicate things just now."

"And I'll also thank you not to complicate it," says Jackson. "Why don't you disappear while I introduce Miss Amanda?"

Jeb sighs and slinks away as a well-dressed woman approaches along the platform. She has porters and servants in tow. Amanda wonders why a woman like this would even want to meet her. Why not get one of the supervising maids to do the interviewing and the hiring? She fully expects to end up in the galley kitchen, seeing no one and up to her elbows in pots and pans. Why should this wealthy woman care about talking to her at all?

To her surprise, when Jackson introduces them, the immaculately dressed woman extends her hand.

"This is the woman I told you about, ma'am."

"Charmed, my dear. I understand you are looking for a job."

"Yes, ma'a—" she starts to say but catches herself. She takes a breath and simply says, "Yes, I am." She looks the woman in the eye. Amanda can't quite make herself call the other woman "ma'am." It's a pride thing. She's not sure why. She's a hard worker, and that should be enough.

The woman eyes her cautiously. "And what is your name, young lady?"

"Amanda Grant."

"I see. And do you have experience with this kind of work, Miss Grant?"

"On a train? No. I have not."

The woman nods. "How about as a maid?"

Amanda doesn't want to lie, so she decides to boast of her experience in a different way. She smiles. "Not in the traditional way. No. But I kept a house for a very demanding husband and myself for three years. I think you'll find that I can do the job admirably."

The woman stiffens. She looks at Jackson, who looks away.

"I see."

Amanda looks her in the eye. "If experience as a maid, especially as a maid on a train, is important, then I'm afraid I can't offer that. All I can say is that I've done this kind of work before. I'm good at it, and I very much need the job, so you can be assured that what I do will be done well."

The woman holds her gaze for quite a while. Amanda does not look away, nor does she stare back in any sort of challenging way.

"And where is your husband now?"

"He has passed away, and he left no estate to speak of. I hope that says enough about why I'm here." She smiles and simply tries to hide the lie of her words. Eventually the woman smiles back.

Out of the corner of her eye, Amanda can see Jackson breathe a small sigh of relief.

"I'm not sure quite what to think. But we are leaving soon, and you come highly recommended by Mr. Jackson here. That carries a bit of weight." Her eyes run up and down the young woman. Eyes that judge detail and value, whether they're examining an expensive vase, a cherished painting, or a perspective employee.

"This is an unusual job. I feel obligated to tell you that. Because the train cars are so much smaller than our home, we can't bring along a full staff. Thus, you'll end up doing double duty. Besides cleaning, you'll need to look after the children. You won't be a nanny exactly, but they will require your attention at times, and it's fully expected that you will provide it."

"Yes. I understand. May I ask how old they are?"

"Old enough, dear. Well past diapers if that's what concerns you."

"No … actually, just that I don't have much experience dealing with teenagers."

"Oh, they're not quite there yet. My oldest, Edwin, is twelve. Sophie is barely eight. If those ages aren't a threat to you, I suppose you should do fine." She nods graciously. "The pay is two dollars per week. Can you start immediately? We may depart as soon as tomorrow."

Amanda is taken aback. "Oh. Well, yes, of course I can. Right now, practically everything I own is in two suitcases."

Mrs. Evans nods slowly. "All right then. I suppose we have a deal. We'll take you on to Chicago with us and see how things work out."

Amanda expresses her thanks, with promises to do well. Jackson sends a boy to fetch her suitcases, and she slips into the train car. She is introduced to the cook, an older German woman named Marta. Amanda is surprised to discover that Marta is the only other servant who will make the trip. The old woman rolls her eyes when she discovers that Amanda's never been a maid. But she pours them both a cup of tea and sits down with a list of duties. Within fifteen minutes, they both feel comfortable and realize they'll probably get along just fine. Amanda helps prepare both the dining car and the private cabins for the family's departure in the morning.

Jackson locates Jeb and delivers the news that their quest was a fruitful one. Amanda will not only make her escape from Boston in the morning, but she'll do so in style, and with her first official paying job since she was married.

Chapter 11

Drink

There's an old rooming house in Boston's Back Bay where Victor stayed after graduating from MIT. The place is not extravagant. It has large rooms where men stay four to a room. There are bunk beds and a small shared washroom on the third floor. A three-hole privy stands in the backyard.

During his first stay at the house, Victor saw a mix of students and immigrant workers, plus an occasional older man, perhaps separated from his wife or perhaps never married. Those men didn't spend a lot of time at the house. Most preferred a pub stool to the loneliness of a low-rent home.

Not knowing where else to go, Victor decides to return to that cheap rooming house. He also decides to make the trip by foot, not only to save the cab fare, but also to push himself a bit. He wants to grow stronger and healthier. Getting out and walking is a good start.

The trek from MIT takes him longer than it should, but he plods onward with slow and steady resolve, taking short rests when needed.

He recognizes the woman who answers the door. They discuss price, and he knows enough to ask for the top-floor room. It's usually the last room to fill up, especially in the heat of the summer. That gives him a good chance to be the room's only occupant. After unloading his meager possessions and taking a little nap, he heads back out into the warmth of the late afternoon. Treating himself to a cab this time, he returns to his old neighborhood. He walks to his father's old house, wondering if Eli is still alive.

Victor has written to Eli several times over the years. In all that time he received just one reply. It came in a childish scrawl that confirmed Victor's suspicion that his father was at least moderately literate. He took some comfort in seeing that Eli could at least string letters and sentences together. The letter carried no deeper meaning. There was no reconciliation in its words. It was just an obligatory *hello, good to hear from you, talk to you later* sort of letter.

Victor stands on the front stoop. No one answers his knock. Then he realizes it's Friday, and in Eli's world that means payday. It also means his father, if he's still alive and working, may have some money, and that means it's time for a drink.

Victor chats with some neighbors sitting on a nearby porch and quickly learns that his father is indeed still living at the home.

"Eli has a son?" one of them laughs. "Well dad burn it, how about that? He never mentioned a son, or any family at all!"

Victor asks where his dad spends his drinking hours.

"Two blocks down, then take a left. Check the small pub on the corner."

A pub? Victor thinks as he walks. That's a step up for Eli. Maybe he's too old now to take his cups on street corners and the docks. Drinking in the gutter could be too uncomfortable for old bones.

The pub is nearly empty, but the workday has ended and more men immediately start to trickle in. They come in ones, twos, and threes. He doesn't see his father anywhere. What he does see are broken chairs that have been taped and wired together. An oval mirror on the back bar may once have been grand, but now it's cracked and filthy. Ornate trim has been knocked loose, probably by rushed bartenders hastily placing bottles of rye and bourbon back on the shelves. He's about to leave when he notices the door to the kitchen is propped open. Through that door he sees a glowing wood stove that's missing one of its rear legs. It sits precariously on a stack of three loose bricks. On top of the stove, he notices a huge black pot that steams away like a witch's caldron, its lid dancing atop escaping steam. A deep breath tells him it's lamb stew. There's also the unmistakable smell of fresh biscuits. The pub may look like a total dive, but the food smells wonderful to a hungry man. Victor decides to stay. He orders some of the stew, taking it at a small table near a front window.

Would he like a drink with that?

Victor has not had a drink of alcohol in years, put off by his own father's consumption. But for some reason he orders a beer with his meal. It tastes good going down. And the lightheadedness that it brings helps to wash away his mood.

He's nearly finished eating when three dirty, unshaven men walk in. The one in the center looks like a very old version of his father. The voice confirms Victor's suspicion as the man slaps a silver dollar on the bar and orders a round of whiskies.

Victor orders another beer, then sits and watches Eli for nearly an hour. Eventually, one of the old man's companions says good-bye, then the other. His father remains, alone, nursing a new whiskey.

Victor takes a deep breath and approaches cautiously. "Eli?"

The man turns around, eyeing him suspiciously. "Who wants to know?"

Victor looks him in the eye, holds the gaze for several seconds, then says, "Your son."

Eli looks him up and down. It takes a moment, but there's a flash of recognition, and the lips turn up into a smile. "Why holy jumping mother of fucking Jesus. You are, aren't you? He steps back for a better view. God damn it, look at you!" He moves haltingly then gives into his feelings. He shakes Victor's hand. Victor decides to hug the old man instead, closing his eyes tightly. The old man stiffens but accepts the hug.

"So where the hell you been, Victor? Oh my. It's been so long. Where... where *have* you been?"

The next twenty minutes are tough ones. Victor has so much to say, but it only trickles out in short phrases, vague questions, and small apologies. He thinks Eli should be apologizing, too, for pulling away and out of his life like he did, but they don't speak of it.

How does a man tell his father that he found success, for a time at least, not because of what that father did for him, but in spite of it? How do you tell him that he provided virtually no inspiration, so you had to leave to find it elsewhere?

And how do you tell him that you tried to stay in contact, but that the years of sending and never receiving letters wore you down? So you stopped trying.

How do you tell a man like Eli that he became more of an embarrassment to you than an asset, and that you just sort of drifted away?

Such words are difficult, and maybe unnecessary. It's easier for Victor just to tell stories about the trips he's taken and the strange places he's seen. It's all painfully superficial. It's only as Victor starts to describe his travels to Asia that he seems to have the old man's undivided attention. When he tells of returning to the Atlantic, and to Europe, and of his eventual shipwreck, he holds Eli spellbound.

After some more small talk, the big questions eventually do show themselves, and they demand attention. "So why did you come back here, Victor? What made you come to find me?"

They've both been drinking plenty. Victor is surprised to find that he has an appetite for it. The noise of the bar has become a hazy background blur. He remembers shaking a hand or two. Eli, as a regular here, knows some of the people in the Friday crowd. Most seem surprised to meet a member of his family.

"I guess I came back because you *are* family," Victor admits when they again find a moment of private talk. "I wanted to find you. After what I've been through, I guess family has become a little more important to me. You're all I have."

Eli's beard bobs a little as he nods. "Yes. I can understand that. Glad that you did come to see me, boy, glad you did."

"You know, Eli ...," he can't quite bring himself to call the man *Dad* or *Father*, "I've chased dreams. I guess I don't want to keep chasing them forever. It's like hunting. Remember that one time you took me hunting?"

Eli scrunches up his forehead, trying to recall. "Yes! God damn it, I'd forgotten about that! But, yes, I do." He takes a long sip from his glass. "You got yourself onto a pheasant, didn't ya? Chased that damn bird over hill and dale. I lost you. Hell, boy, you must have run after that damn thing for three hours. Through cornfields, over into the next valley. It kept flitting away, always staying about 200 feet ahead of you. I think you shot every shell you were carrying trying to kill that thing."

Victor laughs. "Yes, I did. And I never did catch up to it."

"Persistent little bastard, weren't you? I knew it right then."

"I guess I was. But I also learned from it. There's a time to quit. There are many things worth chasing, but there's also a time to let things go."

"Aye, I guess that time does always come. So is that where your head is right now, my boy?"

Eli downs the remainder of his drink before answering. "Yes, I think it *is* where I'm at Eli. I'm at a dead end. Life is strange that way." He looks at his father and realizes that everyone goes through a similar epiphany at some time in their lives. For some it happens much sooner than others.

"What was it you were trying to do exactly, boy? Not sure I understand what it is that you're giving up."

Victor takes a deep breath. "You know that I went to college, right?"

Eli nods. "Yeah, I knew that much. I was proud of ya for that. Guess I never told ya."

Victor smiles. "Well, I'm an engineer. My specialty is electricity."

"That a fact? That's a good thing to be working on, my boy. Damn wires keep going up all over the city. Going great guns, ain't they?"

"Yes. It is good to be part of the whole business. But I've been chasing another dream, too."

He explains to his father the concept of radio. It takes several minutes, but Eli seems to grasp the general idea. For a moment, it strikes Victor how strange this is. Eli is an old man, a Civil War veteran, listening to a description of a communication system that could stretch around the globe in ways that telegraph operators of his day could only dream.

By the time he reaches his father's age, the world really will be a remarkably different place.

"So, what you're talking about, boy, sounds pretty incredible. I find it hard to believe. Do you believe it? Or are you quitting this game because you've decided that maybe this radio wave thing is not possible?"

"Oh, I think it's possible all right. In fact I have no doubt."

Eli fiddles with his whiskey glass for a moment, spinning it in place. "Well, I ain't one to give advice, boy, because my advice seldom turns out to be good. But I'll tell you this much. If you *know* something's possible, that ain't the time to give up on it. The time to give up is when it's obvious that something ain't going to work out for ya. See what I'm saying?"

Victor doesn't respond.

"I quit being a husband because I knowed I was no good for the job. Same with being a father, I guess."

He turns to look Victor in the eye. "But you, boy, you're giving up on something that might very well be in your reach. You ain't hunting birds, boy. Maybe you got tired of this here hunt, but that's the wrong damn reason to quit. If you got something you know is good, then you keep going after it, ya hear me?"

Eli takes a long drink then sets his glass down hard. "But what the hell do I know? I'm just an old drunk that ain't never been good at hunting, or fathering, or much of anything. You're a smart boy. I suppose you know when you're licked. So don't let me give you any shit about it."

Victor stays quiet. He's sitting in a barroom that seems filled with failures. And here he is, failing right along with them.

Victor and his dad, getting drunk in the cheapest of cheap pubs. Shutting out the world. Is he just an intruder here? Or is this where he belongs now?

Victor orders a round of drinks. The conversation continues until nearly closing time. Eventually, the subject comes around to Victor's mother.

"A good woman, God rest her soul," Eli says earnestly. "Deserved better than the likes of me."

"She always said so herself, Dad!" Victor winked.

Eli lets out a long, good-natured laugh. "Yes, well, I never stopped her from saying so because I knowed it was true. She did damn well deserve better. You would do well to find such a woman, Victor. Someone who will put up with you for your successes, as well as your failures."

"What do you mean?"

"I mean there ain't no perfect marriage, lad. Either you're failing to meet her expectations, or she's failing to meet yours. Or worse, a man ends up doing so well meeting his wife's expectations that he ain't living up to his own. Or maybe he's never at home because he's working to be the man that everyone else thinks he should be. You're either a familiar failure to your family, or a successful stranger. I don't think neither of them choices works right well. A man needs to end up somewhere in the middle if he's going to be happy."

Victor nods. Just then a man walks past and slaps Eli on the shoulder. It's a gentle, friendly greeting, but Eli teeters a bit from the impact.

"Say Eli ... Dad, maybe we've had enough for—"

"Look, lad, I have a problem with the drink. You know it. I know it. Hell, everyone here knows it. But did you know I gave it up once? And I don't mean for a few days. It was a good six months, boy. I was dry as an old lady's quim." Eli nods smugly at his son's surprised look.

"It's true. Just after you was born. I came back from the war and I realized I'd spent more than two years straight as a damn drunken sot. Spent some weeks in the brig even. Never did tell your mama about that part. But, oh, there were things I did enjoy about being in the service.

"I loved gliding over the Chesapeake on a clear day. I loved looking at them huge striped bass lingering in the calm spots. I also liked watching those nasty little white jellyfish float by. In the summer months it looked like whole clouds of them floating there just under the water!

"And I loved coming out of that almost endless bay and into the wild ocean. Ship rocking like hell. Birds would follow us out for miles. Once I got my discharge, well, it was a few months before I tracked down your mom. You know what I did in that time? I took a job on a cargo ship that had been hired by the government to help with the war cleanup. We went up and down the bay and then the coastline, moving everything from horses to ammo to tents and all kinds of shit. Dead bodies even, though most of them was boxed up. It was hard work, but not all that bad. We didn't have any sort of deadline. Just instructions to find what we could and to move one boatload of surplus after another. We was just cleaning up the mess. Didn't matter how long we took.

"The point is, all I had to do was just watch the scenery and tote the cargo. I loved it. I almost stayed right there. Didn't even have an urge to drink some days. But you know what, boy? I also knew that I had a son. I had you! I had a life waiting for me here, and it was something I wanted to come back to."

95

He blinks a few times. "Even if I wasn't any damn good at it, I wanted to come find it."

"You did what you could, Dad. I understand that."

"Well, thank you for saying that, son. I guess a man always wants to do a good job, even if he don't know exactly how to do it."

Victor turns to his father. "So you found her, then. You found Mom. I know that. I heard all the stories around the dinner table as a kid."

"Yes. I had a rough idea of where her aunt lived. I sent some letters, asked some mutual friends, and eventually I just showed up at her door. Her aunt tried to shut me out, but your mother took me back, the damn fool. I stayed sober for a while after I was back, too."

"So what sent you back to the drink?"

"To my cups? Well, I don't know exactly. Drink is just drink, my boy. It's always there. Always beckoning to ya. It's an escape. So when you want to escape again, that's the easy place to go. A man fails enough, boy, he learns the best ways to escape that failure."

Victor is silent for a moment, looking over the faces at the bar. Finally, he asks the question that's been on his mind for years. "So what was it you were trying to do that you couldn't quite do?"

Eli thinks about this for nearly a minute. The only sounds Victor hears are the sounds of people bidding each other good-bye as the pub prepares to close. "That's a good question. I've asked it of myself many times. I finally decided that I wasn't running away so much as running to something. You know how I said I loved that time I spent on the ships? On the water? That was freedom for me. Total freedom, boy. A married man doesn't have that. The drink, well, I guess she felt like a small taste of freedom. It still is a little bit of freedom every time I do it."

Victor nods. "But why still? You have your freedom now. Your kids are grown. Your wife is gone. You have all the freedom in the world. I know you aren't as strong as you were. But you could go to sea again."

Eli looks at his hands, his face suddenly showing every scar and wrinkle he's earned in his hard-knock life. "Aye, but a man becomes comfortable where he's at, lad. It becomes home to him. I ain't got much, but I got these people. They all know me here. They pretty much like me and I like them. This is what we do together, lad. We escape together. We drink together. It's what sailors and us dock bastards have always done. This is home, lad. Do you understand? This is home."

Victor, having been welcomed into this home of Eli's, stays until the pub closes. He walks his father home.

Head spinning, feet unsure of their steps, he slowly walks to his own rooming house. His hands are thrust deep into his pockets.

Chapter 12

Departure

Promptly at 7:00 a.m. Mrs. Evans arrives at the train station with her two children in tow. The daughter, an energetic eight-year-old, runs ahead of the pack, whistling and skipping down the platform. The back side of her yellow curls bounce high above the blue bow that pins them back from her face. The girl slows as she approaches Amanda and looks up at her with a grin.

"Are you the new lady?"

Amanda looks at the cook, then down at the girl. "Me? Why, yes, I guess I am the new lady."

"Mother said we would have a new lady on this trip. I didn't expect you to be so pretty."

Amanda blushes. "I … um … well, thank you. And you must be …?"

"Sophie!" She extends her petite hand and offers a perfect handshake, followed by half a curtsy. "Pleased to meet you, ma'am!"

Amanda suspects the girl has learned her manners quite properly, probably in a child's etiquette class.

"How charming to meet you, too, Sophie! I think we'll have a lot of fun on this trip."

"Oh, I know I will. I always do. I love traveling and looking out the window. Did you know we even have an outside platform in the back of the last car? It has chairs and everything!"

"No, I didn't know that. I've only been in the first car so far."

"Come on! I'll show you! Oh, and Mother just bought me a new board game, too! Would you like to play it with me?"

"Well, I don't know. I certainly will if I can." Amanda realizes that she's not entirely sure of her status. Is she supposed to be seen and not heard? If she's to be part nanny, then certainly playing games with the children must be part of the deal, but she doesn't want to ignore her other duties.

"You know what, Sophie? I'll have to check with your mother first, but I'm sure we can arrange something." She winks at the girl, who immediately dissolves into a wave of giggles.

It's a bit harder for Amanda to get a good read on Sophie's older brother. Edwin looks sullen and distant as he walks up the platform. Despite the porters who follow the family with huge stacks of luggage, Edwin carries his own suitcase, plus a small bundle tied with a blue string. He looks at his shoes as he walks, unwilling to engage in the slightest of pleasantries with his family, the staff, or any railroad workers.

"Good to see you, Mrs. Grant." Mrs. Evans nods to the cook as she climbs aboard. "Sophie and Edwin, please go to your rooms to unpack your things."

Sophie changes the subject. "How did your husband die, Mrs. Grant?"

"Oh, he was … he was traveling," Amanda says vaguely.

The porters carry the remaining luggage to the far end of *The Duchess*, loading it into a small door. Every one of the helpers, be they hired staff or the station's porters, suddenly scurry to a pre-assigned place, leaving Amanda standing alone on the platform. She walks to Marta's side, asking what it is she's supposed to do now.

"The men will bring cartons of food and supplies. For now, just help me unload them. After that, we'll see how things go. Just relax."

She assists for nearly an hour. Before the train pulls out, Albert Jackson stops by to see how Amanda is working out. Mrs. Evans smiles and slips some money into his hand. Amanda sees the transaction through the window. It makes her feel good. A tip for Albert Jackson means that Amanda has passed some kind of test.

Before he leaves, Jackson stops at the open window of the car and calls out to her. He hands her a small note. It's from Jeb. The note says that he's arranged to hitch a ride on a train that leaves just after hers. He'll catch up to her soon.

The Evans family's two coach cars are attached to the rear of a thirteen-car train. It turns out of Boston and heads southwest at roughly forty-five miles per hour. It will cross central Massachusetts and a good chunk of Connecticut before entering the lower edge of New York State.

The only car behind the Evans family's private coaches is an old caboose. It's a rusty, rattling, wooden thing, dragged along a bit like Edwin, an errant child who doesn't want to be part of the group.

Everything seems to go smoothly. Amanda helps serve the family dinner, learning quickly to widen her stance as a way to keep her body steady against the swerve and sway of the train. She also learns that Mrs. Evans is extremely formal, both in the way dinner is served and the way she expects the help to interact with her family. Yet the woman seems polite and friendly to her workers—as long as they properly play their servant roles.

Serve from the left, take from the right. Amanda knows that much. If Mrs. Evans addresses her, keep the conversation businesslike and to a minimum. Answer all questions directly. Smile at the kids. Well, at Sophie anyway. Edwin looks at his food and says very little to anyone.

After the food is cleared, Amanda helps clean up the galley. But she's called away by Mrs. Evans, who sits doing needlepoint in the middle of the car. "Sophie wants to know if you'll play her new game with her."

"Of course. I'd love to." She turns to Edwin to ask if he'd like to join them.

"No," he says.

"No, thank you," Mrs. Evans corrects, without looking up.

"No, thank you. I'm busy." He's seated at a desk that's obviously used by his father when he travels with the family. A large green blotter covers the middle of the mahogany top. Edwin draws cartoon characters right on the blotter until his mother notices and tells him to stop.

Amanda and the young girl play the game until about eight thirty, at which time her mother announces that she has to get ready for bed. Amanda returns to the galley for fifteen minutes, then goes to tuck Sophie into her tiny bunk.

"I had a great time!" The girl smiles. "Did you like that game?"

"Why, yes, I guess I did." Amanda smiles. She actually found the game trivial and dull, but Sophie's effervescent company helped to make it a very enjoyable time.

"Maybe we can play it again tomorrow after we look out the windows for a while?"

"Maybe we can," Amanda responds, giving the girl a pat on the head.

Returning to the main parlor, she offers to tuck Edwin in, too. He brushes her offer aside. "I've been putting myself to bed for two years."

And then she's done with her duties. A sudden awkwardness sets in. She can't exactly pour herself a glass of water and join Mrs. Evans. But the car isn't so large that she can stay out of everyone's way.

She nods and slips away, keeping herself busy by straightening and re-straightening the galley for a bit. Then she retires to her bunk, which is in the back of the car, directly across from Marta the cook's berth. Marta lies in her bunk, reading by lamplight. Amanda realizes she should have brought a book of her own.

"At Grand Central, we'll be linked to the rear of a longer train," the cook whispers. "Sometime around 3:00 a.m., I should think. No one needs to wake up and do anything, but there will be several noisy bumps as the car is decoupled and moved."

"So we'll probably all wake up."

"Indeed. I know that I always do. Just wanted to warn you so that you're ready for it."

Amanda sits on the edge of her bed. "How many trips like this have you made?"

"This will be my fourth. I cook for the family at their home, too."

"Do you like traveling?"

"I liked my first trip, dear. After that, such trips get to be pretty taxing. But at least Sophie keeps us all smiling."

"Yes," Amanda whispers, "she's a gem, isn't she?" Amanda drops her voice even lower. "But what's going on with young Master Edwin? He seems terribly pensive and out of sorts."

"Yes. He's been that way for months. I don't know rightly what his issue is, but I do know he doesn't see his father much. The man seems to have no time for him at all. Mostly the lad spends time around women—his mother, the maids, and house help. I don't think he's happy about the situation. He told me once he just wanted someone to play baseball with. There's no one in the whole neighborhood for that, much less on these trips."

"Poor boy."

"Yes, poor him. Maybe. But once you get to know Edwin, it's hard to feel sorry for him for very long. You'll see."

Amanda pulls back the covers on her bed and starts to undress. She sees a motion out of the corner of her eye. She sees a figure, about Edwin's size, duck into the shadows at the back of the parlor. It spooks her, and she stops what she's doing, climbing under the covers while still wearing much of her clothing. She finishes undressing there.

Chapter 13

The Ring

It's not the worst hangover Victor's ever experienced. But it's probably among the top three. Head pounding, stomach in knots, he stumbles into the rooming house kitchen, grabs the largest mug he can find, and pours himself a coffee. Rich and black, it smells like moist earth.

He drinks it on the back porch, squinting against the harsh sun and looking in the general direction of Boston Harbor. That's where his father worked. That's where Eli played and where he drank.

The hangover painfully reminds Victor that this is also how his father woke up on far too many mornings.

As he sips from the heavy cup, Victor decides to head across the back yard, walking directly toward the rear fence. He wants to examine an old bicycle he's seen sitting there for several days. Looking closer, he realizes the two-wheeler must have been parked there for more than just a few days. The chain is rusty and vines have grown around the frame.

Back inside, he asks the rooming house manager about the bike and is told it's been parked there for at least two months.

"Belonged to a previous tenant who never came back to claim it," the landlord shrugs. "It's not in great shape. It's yours if you want it.

So, between sips of coffee and a little near-vomiting, Victor slowly clears away the vegetation, hacksaws through a small lock, loosens up the back gear, and lubes the bike chain. A few adjustments are needed to the rear wheel, which may be why the previous owner gave up on it. But in the hands of an engineer, even an electrical one, the bike is deftly urged back to working order.

Victor had a cousin who used to call these "velocipedes." This velocipede turns out to be a Swift Safety Bicycle, maybe five years old.

At least it's not one of those silly high-wheel bikes. This is the newer style—level, strong, and slick. A decent find, even though it will soon need some new rubber on the front wheel.

After a test lap around the block and a few more adjustments, the first trip Victor takes is over to MIT, to visit with Professor Alton. He lugs the bike into the lobby of the building to park it, then heads upstairs.

His old mentor greets him at his office door. "Victor! Good to see you. How are the wounds? Healing well?"

Victor shrugs. "The healing is slow, but I guess it's happening. I'm grateful for that." He pulls at the loose folds of his shirt. My bigger concern is my weight. I lost a lot in those days when I was unconscious, and then even more right after. Had no appetite."

The professor nods. "Clearly, it takes time to recover. Patience, as you know, is an overlooked virtue."

"Well, I'm running out of patience professor. Just can't seem to build my bulk back up. I'm finally eating like a horse again, but I'm gaining weight like a damn chipmunk."

The old man laughs, jokes about how many people would like to have that problem. Then he thinks for a moment. "Nutrition. Growth. Yes, indeed. New theories about that, you know. Interesting times, right now."

Victor leans against the wall of Professor Alton's office. Through his shirt he can feel the coolness of the enamel-clad blocks. "I'm sorry, sir. Growth? What are you going on about?"

Professor Alton takes off his glasses and cleans them. "Sorry. You know how it is at universities. We talk about and investigate so many things. And we get to hear about what others are working on. It's not really my subject area, you understand. I'm a physicist. So I don't have much expertise in biology."

Glasses back on his head, he looks at Victor. "This growth research… okay… there's a doctor I'm aware of. He's nearby. Over at Harvard. Apparently he's been researching other bodily fluids, and by that I mean that there are things in the human body besides the usual blood and urine and such. Turns out there are many things stored up in, or created by, the human body. So many things that never really have been measured before. He's done a good deal of research and has some interesting ideas."

"I see. What sort of ideas?"

"Well, for one thing, thoughts on what helps with the healing process within the body, and what causes growth, too."

Victor nods. "Okay. So… what made you think of that?"

He points at Victor's head. "Well, he's looking at the thyroid gland, and focusing on health problems related to what some doctors call hyperthyroidism. That part of his theory, well, I guess that doesn't really affect you. But in the process of doing his research, he's been trying to isolate certain growth hormones. Guess they're best described as something that can help with the healing process. Something that can help restore muscle. To build it up.

"Interesting," says Victor. "I'd say if he could perfect such a thing he'd be quite a rich man. People would flock to his door."

"Yes, well, he's not nearly so far along as he'd like to be. So far he's only done some tests. But I've been watching this man's work, Victor. Watching it with keen interest, and I think he may have some ideas that can help you. It's apparent that he's a firm believer in what he's discovered. He believes that these things, these fluids, or hormones or whatever they are, can help promote healing."

Professor Alton looks at Victor, studying the young man's skinny frame and his damaged and wandering eye. "You know what? Let me give you his name. It's Dr. David Burke. He and his colleagues call their study endocrinology. I can't say how much, if anything, he can do for you."

Alton writes a name and address on a piece of paper. "Pay him a visit. He may just be worth your time. "

It's close to 3 o'clock when Victor knocks on the door of Dr. David Burke. When the doctor answers, Victor explains his situation and discovers that Professor Alton already sent a telegram explaining the situation.

"Ah then, pleased to meet you sir!"

Victor shakes hands with a fidgety, awkward, but intensely bright middle-aged man. After a few other pleasantries, he asks about the doctor's work.

"Oh, yes yes yes. Fascinating stuff. Really really intriguing. I could go on and on. But, please, please, first tell me what you want to know, and why?"

"Well, let's start with what you're doing." Victor stares at him for a moment. "Okay, so what is this human growth research that the professor finds so intriguing? He seems to think I should talk to you to learn more."

Dr. Burke strokes his beard. "Okay. Okay. I see. Yes, well, my first goal was, and I guess still is, to carry on the work of two men. The first, Robert Graves, analyzed and described thyroid problems over 55 years ago. The thyroid secrets a substance that we don't fully understand yet, but we do know that it can influence the body's metabolic rate, or, more simply, its energy level. Energy, energy! That's the key, you know! That's the ticket to understanding what's going on! Though it also plays a part in protein synthesis…"

"All right," says Victor, very unsure where things are going.

"Sorry. Sorry. I diverge sometimes. So interesting to talk about this. Anyway, the second man whose research I followed was named Arnold Berthold. He did a lot of work trying to understand testicles, of all things! Go ahead. Make as many jokes as you'd like. I've heard them all."

"No, no," said Victor. With just a slight chuckle. "Go on. I'm listening. Professor Alton says your work is important."

"Well, one thing Berthold discovered, several years ago actually, is that the testicles of a typical male secrete things besides just sperm. That means, besides being used to have fun and to make little people, the testes produce something else that we can't quite isolate, but which seems to have a major impact. Is it a fluid? Some kind of signal? It provides connections of some type, it seems. We don't really know. That's what I'm studying. So much more work needs to be done, and I'm proud to be a part of it."

"So why did Professor Alton want me to talk to you?"

"I… well… I've been running some tests. Squirrels at first. Then pigs. Then I even convinced several prisoners to let me try things on them."

"Things, hum? What kind of things?"

"Injections! Shots. Whatever you like for the name. It's my firm belief that placing these fluids, these substances, based on various sterols, well… I do believe they can promote healing."

Victor looks stunned. "I, um . . . I don't think so, Dr. Burke. I'm not looking to be someone's lab experiment."

"Oh, no, no. We're far beyond experimental. I can assure you. Yes, yes. The prisoners did just fine. They had several weeks' worth of shots. No harm done. None at all."

Dr. Burke struggles with what to say next. "They did… well, I'd say they did even better than expected. They grew strong. They grew, well, larger." The doctor tilts his head and shrugs, like even he can't believe it.

"How so?"

"Their level of energy jumped. They worked harder. The results showed in their bodies."

Victor looks at him, skepticism clearly visible on his face.

Dr. Burke looks back. "You were a healthy and strong man, I take it. You look like you must have been. But you don't look well now. Sorry to say that."

Victor shrugs.

"I suspect that's why Professor Alton sent you to see me, no?"

"It is."

"Come over to this window."

When they look out they see a man working in a small park across the road. He lifts and carries large flat stones, placing each in front of a group of masons who are building a new walkway.

"That man has been out of prison for five months now. Six months ago, he could only lift stones half that size."

"Increasing a little each day helps, I suppose."

"My treatment helped him even more."

"Is that right?"

They watch the man walk back to the stone pile. For the next trip he carries two stones, one under each arm.

"Professor Alton sent you here because he thought I could help you, Victor. And I do believe I can."

Victor remains silent for several minutes. Then his hand moves instinctively to his forearm, which remains undernourished. "Okay," he says at last. "I'm listening."

They discuss the idea for several more minutes. After many assurances, Victor eventually agrees to try Dr. Burke's medicinal cocktail on his next visit.

By the time he returns home, Victor's appetite has returned. At least a bit. He eats a healthy dinner with others at the rooming house. Broiled chicken. Mash potatoes, gravy, and peas. If nothing else, this big house serves decent food.

Some of the other men start to talk about a boxing match scheduled for the early evening. It's supposed to take place in a warehouse down by the docks.

"They put some posters up just yesterday morning," says Thurman, one of few men in the house who Victor has talked with several times. "John L. Sullivan is supposed to be there, can you believe that? Yup, John L. The man himself."

"Bah," someone replies. "Sullivan's getting old. Must be, what, over 30 now?"

"He's still the gloved boxing champion of the world," says another of the housemates. "Guess he's young enough to still be hanging onto that title!"

They talk for a moment about the merits of gloved versus bare-knuckled boxing.

"Well, I don't know anything about titles," says Thurman. "But he's supposed to be taking on Paddy Ryan. And tonight they're doing it the old way. Bare knuckles."

"Ain't them sort of matches illegal now in Massachusetts?" Someone asks. "Supposed to be gloves only here now."

They all shrug. No one is quite sure.

"They put on a good show there. I've been before," says Thurman. "It's not just boxing. We may even get to see some women."

Eventually, five of them head down the street. After paying twenty-five cents they gain entry to an underground fight that will feature several matches plus the great John L. Sullivan's possibly illegal return to bare-knuckle boxing.

The event starts with two lightweights. Barely more than boys, they battle almost to a draw until the very end when one knocks the other down twice.

Then two topless women enter the ring and start to swing at each other. There are many hoots and hollers and a spray of beer in their direction. The brunette one is eventually declared the winner even though it's obvious the whole match is just for show. A girl with just a bodice, stockings, and a split skirt walks by hawking cigars and crackerjacks. By now, smoke hangs heavy in the large room. Mixed with the humidity, it becomes hard to breathe.

There are two more fights, then a midget comedian climbs into the ring to tell jokes about the Boston mayor, and a few about the Pope. In due course, one of the topless women comes back out and picks him up, carrying him off while he pretends to scream for help.

There are a couple good mid-card fights, including a title fight for a New England middleweight champion. Finally they get to the main card. The crowd roars when

John L. Sullivan comes out to fight, and it's difficult to see him at first because of all the hands and hats in the air.

Victor feels inspired even though Sullivan looks heavy and out of shape when he appears.

It's more of an exhibition than a title fight. Eight men are lined up to have a go. Sullivan, with his waxed mustache, trademark full-stretch pants and starred belt, takes on the challengers one at a time. The men fight with a promise of $125 if they win. Some swing with wild abandon while others punch hard and methodically.

But none even come close to really challenging the champ. He fends off their punches with ease and hits back with quick shots every time there's an opening. It's a skill that comes only after many fights.

Number six in the group looks like he has the best shot, twice knocking Sullivan back against the ropes. But the fighter rallies and bulls his way back, leaning into a series of hits that land with terrific thuds. Oohs and ahhs abound from the crowd. Sullivan hammers the challenger back across the canvas until they reach the far side, then he punches his way to a victory, hitting the man hard again and again with his heavy Irish hook until a deft kidney punch causes the man to drop to his knees.

Victor cheers along with the rest of the crowd. Beer spills onto the cement floor and smoke hangs ever lower in the big room. Yes. Just like that. The big man proved that he's still a winner.

Victor realizes that's what he wants, too. He has a tough challenge right now. He's been on a tough road for a while, and he desperately needs a win.

And that's when he makes his decision. It's time to fight in his own way. It's time to be strong again. It's time to win. Yes, he'll take the medicine from Dr. Burke. He'll be the research subject. Just this time.

The air stinks of sweat and sawdust. It's too noisy to hear the voice of someone standing just a foot away. But there's a grin on Victor's face as he and his friends tip the beer man in the corner and buy another round. The taste is sweet and foamy and full of promise.

Chapter 14

Goods

Folded newsprint pinwheels over a sidewalk, rustling lightly before it lands in an outstretched left hand. The hand is pale and wrinkled, yet surprisingly spry in its grasp.

After catching his late evening newspaper, Jonathan Morgan tucks it under his arm, holding it tightly against his gray coat. His other hand flips a quarter back toward the newsboy.

"Keep the change," Jonathan Morgan calls out to the lad.

The newsboy jumps high to catch the coin, losing his tweed cap in the process. Using his teeth, he nips at the metal, judging its authenticity. "Thank you very much, sir! Good evening to ya!"

Beverly Morgan holds Jonathan's arm as they walk down the street. He flips through the paper's first few pages, checking the main news of the day, then the business section, then the sports.

"I wish you'd just buy that thing on the way home," she says, "instead of when we're on our way out for the evening!"

"I can't, blast it. He's usually sold out by then."

The Morgans turn the corner onto a street in Boston's North End, just as Jonathan Morgan reaches the local news page. What he sees there causes him to emit a loud chuckle.

"Well I'll be damned," he says, stopping to point out an article. "Looks like they finally caught up to that Chen Lu character."

"Jonathan, please! If you have to say anything, can you please say *darned* instead of that harsh word? You don't sound like a proper gentleman."

He snorts and points again to the paper.

"I'm sorry. Who are you talking about?" Beverly asks absently. She's looking down the street toward a row of small restaurants.

"Remember that strange little oriental curiosity shop that Jasper and his friend Charles like to visit now and then?"

"You mean the one they took Amanda to when she was looking for help with that puzzle box?"

"Exactly. Looks like the police finally raided it."

"Really? What do you mean 'raided'?" She stops to look over his shoulder. It's a short article with an artist's sketch. "Why in the world would they raid it?"

Jonathan reads the article again. "Stolen goods, apparently. You know, Charles told me he suspected as much the last time he visited that shop. He said the old shopkeeper offered such a variety of items that Charles said it looked more like a pawnbroker than an antiques shop. My guess is the place has been selling stolen items right out in the open for some time." He shakes his head. "Now that's pretty foolish."

"Oh my. Stolen? Do you suppose he had anything to do with our break-in?"

Jonathan refolds the paper as they continue their journey. "I don't know. That's a very good question. It is certainly suspicious that our break-in happened shortly after the three of them went to visit that shop, isn't it? It's always been suspicious to me why the thief who broke into our place seemed to be looking mostly for that box. They didn't take much else."

"Well, good riddance to that box," Beverly retorts, "and to that Chen whatever man, too, if he really was selling stolen goods."

Jonathan barely hears her words. "Perhaps I should pay a visit to the police station tomorrow. Maybe they'll let me take a look at the items they found in the raid."

Beverly shakes her head. "Why would you want to do that? We don't need the box now that … that woman is gone."

Jonathan shrugs. "I don't know. I guess I just want to see why it might be so valuable. Humor me, woman! I think it's worth taking a look."

Beverly looks exasperated, but she decides to hold her tongue for now.

Chapter 15

`Mail`

The train cars do bump roughly and loudly once they reach the back yards of Grand Central. Amanda rises to look out the window, walking into the main part of the car and gripping one of the bolted marble tables to steady herself. She sees other cars being pushed toward the back of the yard. Once they are out of the way, the long skyline of New York City begins to reveal itself to her. Some of the buildings must be twelve stories or more in height. She stares at the lights of the buildings and the shadows of people moving about in the night. The city sights keep her enthralled for more than ninety minutes. The more she looks, the more she seems to see.

This is the very reason she decided to travel. Even in the dark, this is the sort of thing she's seen only in magazines.

Their private car is attached to the rear of another train. They pull away from New York just before sunup, heading south toward Washington, DC. That's where they will pick up Mr. Evans. Then it's on to Chicago.

The trip from Washington to Illinois will take about two days. For the first, they'll be hitched to the back of a Chesapeake & Ohio passenger train. For the second day, they'll be part of a group of cars belonging to the Illinois Central Railroad. Amanda has been told that they will stay in Chicago for a week—the family with relatives, and the hired help remaining on the train, parked in a leased space at the far end of a rail yard. When the week is done, they'll head back home, probably via Cleveland.

The Evans' parlor car is attached to the rear of a large mail car. With locked doors and no public aisle through its center, the mail car effectively isolates the private cars from the passenger coaches, keeping the riffraff at arm's length.

In the corner of the rattling, cold mail car sits an old metal army cot, bolted to the wooden wall to keep it from tipping or sliding. On this cot rests Jeb Thomas, staring at the ceiling, watching moonlight twist and snake above him as it shines through the passing trees.

The reshuffling of trains in New York allowed him to catch up with Amanda, and he went to great pains to make sure he was given free passage on a mail car that would be attached to her train. It was an extra bonus to discover that his mail car wound up just one car away from where she sleeps.

He's practically bursting at the seams to let her know that he's there, but he obviously can't awaken the family to say hello.

For now he just sits and stares at the ceiling, smiling a devilish little smile to himself.

Chapter 16

Juice

The so-call sterol alcohol compound stings a bit when it's injected. But the process is far easier than Victor expected.

"That's all there is to it?" He looks at his arm jut as the needle slides out.

"Yes. Of course. Not complicated at all," says Dr. Burke. "At least not for the administration of it."

Victor rolls his shirtsleeve down. "So what happens next?"

The doctor shrugs. Maybe nothing. Maybe in a day or so you'll feel different. It's not like an instant boost of energy. It's more about stamina. When you work your muscles, you will be able to work them longer, and maybe a bit harder. You won't tire quite as quickly, and that will make a difference as you exercise. All of that adds up to help build muscle, but it takes days and days.

"I don't need to do anything else?

"Eat! If you feed your muscles, and feed them well, they will grow. At least, that's what we've seen in others who have used this treatment."

Dr. Burke gives him some instructions and background information and tells him to return later in the day. On his way out, Victor notices a group of workmen disassembling part of the interior of a large clock tower across the street. On the sidewalk sits a crate holding a brand new clock mechanism. The face of the new clock looks as big and round as a dinner table. Beside it are some of the pieces of the old clock, including some rusty mounting brackets.

Victor eats a hearty lunch back at his rooming house, then decides to take a spin on his bicycle. After nearly two hours of riding, including a trip to Bunker Hill and then a separate trip up Beacon Hill, he realizes he's had more exercise in a single afternoon than he's had all week. Yet, he feels fine. Perhaps Dr. Burke was right. The medicine is more about improving stamina. The muscle gain and strength is kind of a side effect.

He returns to Harvard a little after 4 o'clock and receives a second injection. Dr. Burke assures him that what he experienced while riding his bike is normal, and that he should continue to eat hearty and healthy meals.

"Get plenty of sleep, too, Victor. With so much exercise, your body needs to repair itself."

As he leaves the office, he sees that the new clock has been uncrated and hauled up into the tower. Parts of the old clock have been lowered to the street. Gears, weights, and the long clock arms sit on the edge of the gutter, along with the decayed wood of what used to be the old clock face. Victor stops to look at the pile as the workmen load up their cart.

"What are you going to do with these old parts?" he inquires.

"What, this lot?" one of the workmen replies. "We'll probably dump the heavy stuff in the river. No one wants old broken clock parts."

Victor eyes two brass gears that are about the size of trash can lids. "What about those?"

"I don't know. Yours if you want them. Brass has a bit of scrap value, but it's tough to find a buyer."

Victor does indeed want them. But not for their scrap value. Nodding his thanks, he lifts them, one under each arm. They must weigh close to 30 pounds apiece.

It's exhausting to carry the load back to his rooming house. But he only needs to stop a couple of times to rest. Once he arrives, he carries them to the back yard. Sorting through a pile of scrap lumber in the alley, he pulls out a fat wooden dowel that used to be a handrail from a staircase. It easily slides through the center holes of the gears. Using a few nails and a brick, he manages to balance them at either end of the stick. Now he has his own makeshift set of barbells. The dowel flexes a bit too much, so he sisters in some strips of wood and tapes them in place. It's fat and awkward, but it will do the trick.

He only has enough energy left to hoist the barbell a couple of times, but he's satisfied that the weight will help get his upper body in shape, just as the bike is helping with his legs.

That night he sleeps the deepest sleep he's felt in many weeks.

Chapter 17

Work

The next morning Victor Marius sends a telegram to his friend and mentor, Nikola Tesla. He also sends one to his former boss at Westinghouse.

"If there's a response to either message, please just hold them here," he tells the clerk. "I'll be back to pick them up later."

Victor keeps himself busy for most of the day, reading the classified sections of newspapers and fixing up his room. He finds some old pictures in the attic and he gets permission to hang them on his wall. Then he goes to a secondhand clothing store and buys two pairs of pants and two shirts. Back at the rooming house, he hangs them in the closet and marvels at how lonely they look there. He also puts some new underwear in the drawer of an ancient orange chest.

So far he has not been assigned a roommate. Others seem to prefer being on the lower floors. When the room becomes oppressively hot, he opens all the windows on the top floor and most of the ones on the lower floors, too. It helps to get a breeze circulating through the house, forcing stale air up and out.

With no one else around, he strips off the restricting vest. Dropping to the floor, he tries to do a pushup. With great difficulty he manages one. The rods attached to his damaged arm help steady him. He drops down to try another and fails to get more than halfway up. He rolls over and looks at the ceiling.

"Tomorrow," he says, through gritted teeth. Two tomorrow. And three the next day."

After a couple of minutes he strips the rods from his arm and goes through a series of stretching and lifting exercises. He keeps it up until the arm seems heavy and dull, then he reattaches the rods.

"More of that tomorrow, too."

Returning to the telegraph office around five o'clock, he finds only a telegram from Westinghouse. The reply says they won't need his services immediately, but they may have an opening for him in a few weeks. Dejected, he shoves the telegram into his pocket.

"Tell me something," he asks the clerk. "Where do men find work in Boston?"

"What do you mean? What kind of work?"

"Quick work. Labor work. Anything. If any bloke off the street wants to hire himself out for a day or a week, where would he go to do that?"

"Well. Let me think." The clerk motions for Victor to follow him to the front door.

"You see that intersection about four streets down? Take a right there, then go down another two blocks. I walk past there every day and I've seen men gather on that block in the early morning. It's a busy intersection. Supervisors who are in charge of construction projects, freight hauling, or trash removal—anything like that—they sometimes pull up to that corner in their wagons. They offer a few dollars for a few hours of work."

"So that's where you'd go?"

"Well, that's where I'd go it I wanted to haul dirt or swing a hammer. But I'm pretty happy right here."

"I don't suppose you need any help here, do you?"

The clerk shakes his head no.

Three days later, three days of exercise behind him, Victor rises before the sun. He feels stronger. He coughs less. He feels strong enough after he tightens his leather vest around his bruised midsection. He also wraps a makeshift leather brace around his bruised arm and tucks it under his shirtsleeve, out of sight. He dresses in some older clothes that he bought from a rag picker and makes the trek up to the place where the workers gather. Eight other men mill about. None of them seem to know each other. One carries the tools of a carpenter. Another has two cement trowels. The rest, like Victor, carry nothing other than a lunch sack.

Two wagons pull up, then two more. The men driving the wagons seem to recognize some of the men, and they're the first to be chosen. Soon Victor stands alone, then another man walks up and leans against a lamppost.

"Been here long?"

"Maybe fifteen minutes."

The other fellow nods. "Been slow this week. Not much out there." He looks Victor over. "Ain't seen you out here before."

"No. My first time."

"Well, shit, that's just what we need. More damn competition."

127

Victor laughs it off. "What can you do? Times are tough."

"Yeah, tell me about it. I ain't had full-time work in over a year. Things been getting better, though. Guy I worked for last week said he may have something that will keep me busy for the next six months. Big water pipeline going through the south side. He usually don't come here looking for workers until after eight or so. Maybe he'll come today."

"Think he needs more men?"

"Don't know. I'll ask him. I got first choice at it though."

The pipeline foreman does pull up about ten minutes later. He hires both of them and promises to keep them busy for several days if they promise to show up every day. Both quickly agree.

As an engineer, Victor does not find the pay lucrative, but it will help pay his bills for a while. The first day is a long one. The wheelbarrows full of dirt are exhaustingly heavy. The pick and shovel work is grueling. By midday, Victor feels too weak to handle such a load, but he has no choice. The support around his arm does less good with each passing hour. He finds a short, flat piece of wood and ties it into place on the other side of his arm to give his wounded muscle some additional support. He can't stop working, especially since he's found a job that will last several days. Maybe more.

At the end of the day, and at the end of the next day, too, he staggers home and falls lifelessly into his bed. On day three, the group puts in an extra-tough morning, rolling pipes into the ditches with huge crowbars, then re-covering them with dirt once they're attached together. The foreman takes pity on the crew and provides a free lunch for everyone. It's a big pot of chicken soup from a nearby rooming house, plus brown bread and some bitter cheese. Victor eats heartily. He's finally growing stronger. He can feel it.

The work is tough, but the fresh air and the exercise do him good. When he returns home, he finally picks up a razor. Most of the whiskers go. But he leaves the mustache.

New life. New look. And the hair helps cover some scars on his upper lip.

He checks the telegraph office every day, but there's no reply from Tesla. Victor sends another telegram, and also a separate message through a mutual friend, Ben Grady, at Westinghouse. A reply comes back from Grady the next morning.

TESLA NO LONGER AT THIS FACILITY [STOP]

STILL DOING SOME WORK FOR W, BUT MOSTLY PURSUING OWN EXPERIMENTS [STOP]

MAY FIND HIM IN NEW YORK CITY [STOP]

TRY HOUSTON STREET [STOP]

VERY SORRY TO HEAR -W- HAS NO WORK FOR YOU NOW [STOP]

THAT'S GRATITUDE, EH? [STOP]

-- BEN

As Victor heads home, the foundation of a plan starts to evolve in his head. He wants to meet up with Tesla again. He wants to talk with him about radio and ask him for help. Victor needs to refine some ideas. Tesla understands these things. He is one of the few people who believes in the technology.

Neither of them really needs Westinghouse to take that next step, do they?

Victor counts his cash when he gets back to the rooming house. He has enough money to travel to New York and maybe even to rent a room there for a week or so. That's what he'll do. He will go, he'll talk to Tesla, and they'll make some plans for new tests and new refinements. Even if they don't have proper funding, they can make a little progress.

Victor laughs as he strips off his work clothes, pops off the latest brass and leather supports he's built for his chest and arm, and cleans himself at the dry sink with a bowl of water. He trims the mustache, which is coming in nicely.

It's not much of a plan that he's put together, but it's something. Just a few more days of work should be enough, then he'll have the savings he needs to head for New York.

It's been a couple years since he's been there. It will do his soul some good.

Chapter 18

Rumble

Jeb Thomas lies silently on his cot, feeling the bump and sway of the train. The day started with a slight overcast, but by late morning it's become nice and sunny. In two days he has business in Chicago. But for now, his low-budget travel situation leaves him without much to do. So he chooses to rest.

A few hours earlier, Jeb stepped out on the sill of the mail car's back door. After a few minutes, he managed to catch Amanda's eye through the window of the Evans' train car. She was washing dishes at the tiny sink near the front window.

The look on her face was priceless. She knew he planned to catch up with her, but this was much sooner than she expected. She nervously looked around. Did anyone else notice him? She gives him a quick "shame-shame" motion with her finger, and he responds with a wink before stepping back inside the mail car.

Now Jeb waits, and sways, and wonders what the evening will bring. He waits for a sound. Maybe the clank of a pebble on the rear window, anything that will tell him that Amanda is trying to contact him.

Eventually, out of boredom, he explores the mail car. There's a small woodstove at the far end, so he lights a fire and places a half-full kettle on the burner, giving little thought to how long the water has been there. He keeps the fire low so that only the barest wisp of smoke is visible outside. He also uses a makeshift safety feature that's been added to the little stove. A small chain can be draped over the kettle and attached to a hook on the stove's far side, keeping it from rattling off the burner as the train moves.

Many mail sacks lie in a corner. On some trains a mail handler is assigned to the car. There are slots along one wall, and if a handler is along for the ride, he will sort the mail while the train is in route.

Opening one of the sacks, he begins to paw through the letters. There are the usual postcards, some with pictures, some without, and a few with double stereoscopic images of New York on the front. There are all types of letters, some personal and some with business addresses. Whenever he notices a letter addressed to a company that he recognizes as one that does not hire union labor, he sets the letter aside. By the time he looks through four mail sacks, he has six letters in his pile. These will be useful if he needs to restart the fire.

As the afternoon wears on, he grows bored and walks back to the rear door, hoping to catch another glimpse of Amanda.

The anticipation of seeing her again makes him anxious and edgy. He's longed for this moment, not just since the train pulled out of New York, but for weeks. Ever since their meeting at the dance, he's dreamed of her. He's slowly worked to pair himself off with her. By helping her move from her room at the Morgans', and by helping her find this job, he has become her confidant and her friend. Hopefully he also will become her lover.

Ever since that day in the park, before they discovered Amanda's room had been broken into, he's known that she is a special woman. He actually feels guilty that he knows the details of the break-in, and that he will never share that with her. Instead, he dreams of the comfort and softness she seems to offer. He dreams of her smile.

Now she lingers nearby like a Christmas present, tantalizingly close but not yet ready to be unwrapped.

As evening approaches, Jeb paces in the darkening mail car. In the Evans parlor car he sees the family moving around. They eat dinner while he eats an apple and hardtack. The family moves to their parlor chairs while the help cleans up. Eventually the lights dim as the family goes to bed.

Finally, Jeb hears a sound. A low clunk, then a tapping. He rushes to the rear door. Through the small window he sees her, leaning out the door of the Evans' coach. She holds some sort of long stick, reaching across the gap to tap on his window. It turns out to be two mop handles taped together.

Jeb slides open a window on the mail car door and says, "Hi!" It sounds like a stage whisper, barely loud enough to be heard above the rumble of the wheels.

"How do I get over there?" Amanda whispers back. They both look down. The gap is at least seven feet—too far to leap without a running start—and it's dangerous to try to walk over the coupling.

Jeb pulls open his door, grasps a handrail, and takes a step, bravely placing his foot near the edge of the coupling. He stands just shy of the middle spot where the two cars intertwine. "Take my hand!" he urges.

"And then what?"

"Then step across!"

Her eyes widen. "Are you crazy?"

"Well, can I come over there instead?"

She looks over her shoulder. "No! I don't dare to have a visitor!"

"Then you come here. You can do it. I know you can!" He waves in encouragement, drawing her in.

"No ...." White knuckles grip a metal bar mounted near the door of the car. Her eyes lock onto the noisy, dangerous blur that rushes beneath. It's hypnotic.

"Don't look down! Come on, just step forward!"

Amanda shakes her head. "I can't. Maybe you should try to come here instead."

Jeb smiles, but he starts to burn inside.

He can't go to her car. They would have to be too quiet. There would be no freedom there. They have to meet on his side of the gap. That's been his plan since he came aboard.

"We'll wake them if I come over. Come on. Take my hand!"

He stretches out as far as he can. His hand isn't very far from her. He shifts his foot, straining toward her. Aching.

Biting her lip, she reaches back, her foot sliding along on the swaying connection. Their fingers touch. His hand closes around hers like a vice, pulling her toward him. One step. Two. She looks down, studying her feet as they edge across the narrow bridge above the blur of ties, like a tightrope that isn't tight.

The train starts to round a curve. Everything coils, snake-like, to the left.

"Keep coming," Jeb urges.

Once her foot reaches the middle of the squeaking coupling, Jeb gives a powerful tug. She literally flies into him. Into his arms and against his cheek. He starts to spin backward, but they can't move. They both look back and see the hem of Amanda's dress caught on the edge of the hitch. She teeters perilously, and he teeters with her.

Jeb holds her with one arm. Amanda tugs at the dress. No amount of movement shakes it loose. She tenses.

"It's okay. Relax. Look …." He tugs at it, too. But feeling off balance, he quickly grabs the handhold again.

"Come on, just pull forward."

"I can't rip it! I'll be in trouble. It's a borrowed dress!"

But no amount of wiggling shakes it loose. Jeb grabs her by her waist and falls backward toward his car. They both shriek as they hear a low ripping sound. He ends up on his back, with her on top. He looks up to see her smile and presses his lips to hers. The kiss lasts nearly a half minute.

Amanda finally sits up to inspect the damage, but Jeb pulls her back down again. Laughing more. Kissing more. Safe now in the dark. The urgency blurs whatever worry she had over the dress damage. She kisses back. She can taste his hunger, and it's wonderful. She feeds on it, too.

They make their way to his cot and clumsily fall in. She slows him, holding his hands, talking, soothing. They have all night. She knows this. His urgency betrays him, but she can keep it at bay. Stroking his hair, making him talk to her as they slowly undress. They talk of where they're headed. He will not stay with her in Chicago. Instead, he will make his way to the meatpacking plants.

The Evans family have been vague about her duties when they're in the city. At first, they said she would stay with the car. But they have hinted that she may need to come with them to the Chicago apartment.

But for now, she lets him kiss her and slowly drinks in his attentions. His lips find their way to her neck, then nuzzle into her open collar. He unbuttons the front of her dress slowly, kissing lower.

Just as he reaches her bustline, she holds his head, drawing it back to her lips, which he tastes with bliss. "Shhh," she says as he protests. Her hands explore him, too, feeling the breadth of his chest and the curve of his shoulders. Hands dropping slowly to feel him everywhere. The back, the shoulders, the muscles of his arms. Encouraging … slowing. Starting again. Driving him mad.

The train starts up a low incline. A series of clacks echo as couplings draw tight between all the cars. Far up the tracks the locomotive chugs harder, bulling through the weight of its burden on the hill.

Jeb's shirt is off. Then his shoes. Amanda allows him to finish unbuttoning her blouse, feeling his lips explore the top of her bosom. Yes, she wants this. They fall back together into the white sheets.

As they remove the last of their clothes, the train reaches the top of a hill and starts its descent. The speed is dizzying. The rocking of the car prompts them to cling to each other. The metal cot is strong and bears their combined weight with no complaint. But the space is narrow.

Jeb climbs on top of her, struggling to take his pleasure from her surrender. But she squirms, frustrating him. He sees her sly grin, tongue pressed to the back of her lip. She holds him tight. Whispers in his ear. "Tell me what it is that you want."

"You."

"I know."

"All of you."

She demands specifics. He tells her everything, building, hoping, and shivering with lust. She really is a maddening woman.

"Come here, you," she finally says, pulling him toward her and kissing at his chin, then his neck, then the lobe of his ear. He runs his hand up her leg. When he reaches the top of her inner thigh, he stops, feeling her squirm with anticipation. Now it's his turn to tease, slowly moving his hand back down her leg again.

"You ...," she whispers.

"Hmm?" He laughs, nibbling at her nose.

He lets his hand slip upwards again ... suddenly she looks at him.

"Jeb," she asks, rubbing her hands over the muscles of his chest. "Are you happy? Here? With me?"

"Yes," he says with a wink. "Very happy."

She smiles up at him, her face glowing in the moonlight. "I'm so glad we're both here then, on this trip, wherever it is that we are right now. Passing through these hills on this new adventure."

"So am I, Amanda," he whispers as he kisses her.

Outside, the rush of the wind grows louder. The trees sit closer to the tracks along this stretch. Tips of great silver maples slap at the windows as they pass. Then the train exits the woods and crosses a small trestle.

The air is cooler now. It spills into the windows. Amanda thinks of the Evans children back in their bunks, heads tucked beneath wool quilts, bodies curling into the fetal position to keep warm.

But there in the dark mail car, in a small cot in a far corner, Amanda clings to her new man, drawing him to her. Inside of her. Part of her.

She feels the tension in him that she has helped create. She longs to absorb that urgency. His warmth and her own fill the bed. The energy overflows, spilling out and heating the room. Insistent. Beseeching. Arms and legs grasp and release. She wrestles with him, fights his every rise and hastens his every fall. Despite the cold, the taste of sweat hangs on their lips—salty, satisfying, and sweet.

Amanda takes from him. He is surprised at how capably she does so. And he gives—more than he knew he had.

He finds himself wishing for more fortitude. Enough to last all night—a lifetime even. But fury like this can't last. Eventually he falls onto her, exhausted.

There were times when beauty such as hers never seemed available to someone like him. She seems like an object that should be placed beneath glass, or parked behind an art museum's velvet rope. Beauty like this must be seen, but not touched, except by a privileged few.

Does she know that? Jeb wonders as he catches his breath. Does she realize what she truly is? He suspects that maybe she does, but not with full confidence yet. Just a day ago, when talking about working as a maid, she seemed meek and full of doubts. But now, in this rumbling car, she seems to know exactly who she is, what she has, what she can do with it, and what it all might be worth.

Is that kind of confidence something to admire in a woman? Or is it something to fear?

As they linger in their embrace, Jeb also thinks of Amanda's husband and wonders what kind of man he is.

Even as he lies with Amanda, Jeb has a strange sense that he's living on borrowed time. This all can be taken away. He could be left alone, pulled apart by the power of his own longing.

He chooses to push the thoughts away and wallow in the beauty of the moment. It's a marvel, what he sees and feels right there in his hands. Already there are good memories. He remembers her in the park. He sees her eating strawberries. He recalls their dancing in the barn.

And now?

A dirty mail car. A moving train. This, too, is already a cherished piece of their shared history. He wants time to stop. But he somehow wants it to continue on, too. This moment should last forever, but he also wants to finish and begin again.

They talk.

They kiss.

They make a space between them but it doesn't last. Theirs is a consuming passion, warming the air again.

The warmth comes and goes far into the night. Eventually a man and a woman lie asleep in each other's arms. Amanda's shoulders are wrapped tightly beneath Jeb's arm when he is awakened by the low rumble of thunder in the distance. He listens to it spit and sputter for several minutes as it makes its way over the hills, just north of where their train is headed.

He looks down at the face of a sleeping angel and wonders how long it will last. An hour later a light rain taps on the windows. He awakens her, making sure that she is able to return to her car before dawn.

Chapter 19

Gears

Every evening Victor Marius visits Harvard to receive another hormone shot.

"Chemical messengers, lad, that's how these shots really function," says Dr. Burke. "Yes, yes indeed. The endocrine glands normally produce them and they control or influence most bodily functions. Could be as simple as making you feel hungry. Could be as complex as influencing reproduction or changing your mood. We're just adding to what your own body can produce. This set, this experiment, is all about making you feel fit again and getting your muscles to grow."

It always seems strange to Victor that he feels nothing immediately after the shots. It's not at all like taking a drink or smoking a cigarette. The impact comes later.

Every morning he wakes up before dawn and spends at least an hour out in the yard, doing pushups and lifting his makeshift barbell. He's learned that if he yanks the equipment upwards and snaps it in just the right way he can get the big brass gears on the ends to spin a bit, giving the bar a gyroscope effect as he tips it side to side. He's found that this lateral movement helps strengthen the muscles around his damaged forearm.

After working his muscles, he usually runs a mile to the Boston Common and then back again. He's feeling good, he realizes. Even great. The workouts and the injections are really making a difference.

As he jogs back into the yard, he sees Professor Alton waiting for him. The old man waves and holds up a wire frame that contains a series of lenses. "There you are Victor! Come look. I made something for you!"

What he hands Victor looks like a tapered set of magnifying glasses mounted on a swing arm.

"What is it?"

"Something that will help you."

"Okay…"

"It's for your eye Victor. The one that wanders since your accident. You don't have to wear it all the time. But you and I both know that the eye tends to drift to the left as you grow tired. That's why I mounted the lenses on a swing arm. You can swing it down when you need it. And adjust it left or right if you're tired."

Victor tries it and is moderately happy with the results. But he also wonders if he shouldn't just exercise his eye like he's working on the rest of his body.

"So I see you're running now," the professor says. "And apparently lifting weights, too? Feeling good?"

"Feeling fantastic, sir. Better than fantastic. I can't thank you enough for putting me in contact with Dr. Burke. That's made a huge difference."

The professor looks him up and down. "Hum. Yes, well. All things in moderation, right?"

Victor laughs. "If you say so. But me? I'll take these shots every day to feel like this. Quite happy to."

He thanks the professor and tells him he needs to get cleaned up. Once he's back in his room, he takes off his shirt and looks into a mirror. He does indeed look better after just a handful of days, a few shots, and more food than he usually eats; he's heavier, stronger and full of energy. Even his forearms look thicker.

He picks up his squashed leather top hat and attaches Professor Alton's lens to the hatband. The arm is long and curved enough that it reaches around the brim. With a little flick he can lower it down to his eye or flip it up and out of the way.

Back in the mirror, he barely recognizes the man who looks back at him. He looks better than a week ago, yet he looks different than he did before the accident. With the lens in place he looks both strong and strange. He's not sure what to make of it. A bit of anger wells up when he thinks of all he's been through. But he wills it away just as his fist tightens. This is progress. This is good. Don't focus on the anger.

Chapter 20

Visitor

Devlin Richards is out of sorts, and he's not a man who easily endures such feelings. The two main business contacts he's made since coming to Boston, Jeb Thomas and Chen Lu, have both disappeared. Chen is in jail and Jeb has left town.

Devlin's naturally suspicious mind makes him wonder if he's been set up. It's all too convenient. The box disappearing into a locked safe. Chen being arrested then Jeb moving on. Did they steal from him? The two of them working together?

New England Yankees. Chinamen, too. They can never be trusted. Not ever.

The southerner sits in darkness at the edge of the crowd at The Rose Point and seethes. The only thing that keeps him from going after either of them is that he's not entirely sure whether he's been duped.

Devlin is on his second beer when an older man approaches him. He's quite tall with just a hint of Asian features, light brown eyes, and a neatly trimmed head of gray hair.

"You are Mr. Richards, no?"

Devlin says nothing. He simply looks back with malicious indifference.

"I have a message for you. It comes from one that I think you know."

Devlin looks skeptical. "And who the hell might that be?"

"A man who owns a shop here in the city. I'm quite sure you know who I mean."

Devlin offers no invitation to sit, but the man does so anyway.

"This better be worth my while," Devlin says, pulling the candle close.

"I don't know if it will be worth your while or not. I am simply the messenger. I know Chen well enough that I chose to pay him a visit in prison. During such a visit he suggested that I find you here. He said I should talk to you."

"Yeah? And why is that?"

"Apparently the two of you are interested in recovering a missing box?"

Devlin stiffens. "I have no idea what you're talking about."

"Just as I have no idea what's supposed to be in this box, nor do I care. I am simply delivering a message for my friend."

"I haven't heard any message yet, old man. You planning on delivering one or not?"

The older man closes his eyes. He's obviously a gentleman who expects a certain level of politeness within his business conversations. The attitude raises Devlin's ire. It's so typical of these damn Yankees, or whatever this man's background is, Asian or not. Such arrogance. Such privilege.

"Chen Lu says to tell you that it may be possible for you to recover a box."

"Does he now?" Devlin tries to continue his air of indifference, but his attention is piqued.

"There is a police officer, name of Hudson, who patrols an area just south of Boston Common."

"You mean where all the damn Chinamen live?"

The old man raises an eyebrow.

"Yeah, well, what of this Officer Hudson, old man? What is Chen looking for, and why should I need to know about this cop?" Devlin gives no indication that he has met Hudson before.

The visitor places his fingers together, searching for the right words. "Mr. Lu would like you to contact the officer. The man is more of a friend than it might appear. He may wear a uniform, but he is known to do certain favors. At his core he is, like many of us, a businessman." He smiles politely.

"Men like you choose your words far too carefully," Devlin scoffs. "Known to do favors? A businessman? Why can't you just say what you mean rather than dropping hints?"

The gentleman, who looks tall even when sitting down, stares back at him.

"Okay," Devlin continues, "so let's say I do find him? Then what?"

"Simply tell him what you need."

"Maybe I need a lot of different things. And maybe I don't want to get my ass arrested. Sending me to talk to a cop? I don't think so. You setting me up, old man?"

Devlin's knife appears so fast that the visitor wonders whether it's been pointing at him the whole time.

"If I wanted to see you arrested," the old man replies, "it would have been easy enough to bring a policeman with me, no?"

Devlin grunts.

"As I said, I have no desire to know anything more about this item you seek. In fact, it would be unprofessional of me to ask at all."

"Unprofessional? What do you mean by that?"

"I'm an attorney, Mr. Richards. My clients are mostly the Chinese people like Chen Lu who have immigrated to this city in the past ten years or so. There was not much of a Chinese population here before then. Our numbers are still small, but they steadily grow, and we must stick together. Protect each other's business."

"Then why don't you go after the damn box yourself?"

The attorney smiles. "I'm not about to risk my professional livelihood on some wild goose chase. If Chen Lu wants to get that box back, I'm happy to let him deal with a man like you."

Devlin squints. He takes a long lingering look at the attorney. "So where is it?" he finally asks.

"We believe it is in the police station. Whether they were able to remove it from that safe is unclear. Perhaps they brought the whole safe to the station. What we do know is that the police have it in their possession along with many other items from Mr. Lu's shop."

"And should we be able to recover it, what would this cop, this Officer Hudson's role be?"

"He works in that station is all. He has access to things. But whatever deal you might make with him is up to you. My only purpose here is to deliver a message from my client."

Devlin snorts. "So I guess you're done."

The old man nods. "Yes, I do believe I am." With that, he stands and heads toward the door.

"You tell him," Devlin calls after, "you tell that damn Chen Lu that I'll make contact with his man. I'll see what I can do. But I want to know what sort of cut he's expecting now. You understand? I need to know that!"

The attorney doesn't look back. Outside the door he pulls on his hat and heads for the bridge that will take him back to Boston.

Chapter 21

Rooms

As the train pulls into the Chicago train yard at 8:03 a.m., Jeb Thomas finishes reading the last of the mail that he lifted from the mail sacks.

He doesn't drink any of the stale water in the tea kettle that he found, but steam from the pot proves handy for opening some of the envelopes. He reads about a dozen letters and doesn't garner much information, but in his business, even a small bit of news can help. And he does find a ten-dollar bill in one of the envelopes, payment for some transaction between two companies. When he realizes that both are large companies that have had union difficulties in the past, he decides to pocket the ten, figuring it's a way to make them pay for neglecting the working men.

He reseals the letters and returns them to the sacks.

Walking to the window, he sees Amanda's shadow as she moves around in the Evans coach. Her return to the other car had been uneventful. The crossing went better this time as she held her skirt high and stepped across the coupling. By the time the train rolled through the outskirts of the city, she was helping the cook prepare breakfast, setting the table, and preparing to fill a laundry tub once they reached the station.

In her car, Amanda looks out the windows, too. She watches the housing density increase as they roll toward the center of town until the spaces between the homes disappear—until they touch each other and grow taller. Grass turns to sidewalk. Wood siding changes to brick.

At first these stacked residences all seem dark, stained by coal dust and left to atrophy in the Illinois wind. Children, wearing clothes dreary as the walls, hang out the windows, waving at the train. But as the train enters a different neighborhood, the buildings seem to change for the better. They're newer and brighter, with taller windows. Many have bay fronts. She sees flower boxes. A better class of tenant lives closer to the city center. The last things she sees are lovely townhouses with fat trim painted in brilliant colors. Then tall walls suddenly appear beside the tracks, and the view is blocked.

As they reach the train station, Amanda observes a distinguished gentleman waiting at the end of the platform. He checks his watch as the cars squeal to a halt. This must be Mr. Evans, here to greet the family.

He steps aboard the car and wanders into the dining area, saying nothing. He kisses his wife and daughter and then pats the boy on the head. "Hello father," the children say in unison. He sits at the table, immediately opening a copy of the *Chicago Tribune*. Amanda is not introduced, and she realizes that knowing her name or even acknowledging her presence is not part of the protocol.

She quickly brings Mr. Evans' breakfast, which he eats in silence. Edwin, who hasn't seen his father in several days, asks what he's been doing. He receives a quick answer, then the older man sends the lad off into the station to see if he can find a copy of one of the New York or Boston newspapers.

"Even if you find one that's a few days old, buy it!" he commands. "It's better than this drivel."

Amanda brings new plates of eggs and bacon as Edwin returns. The father takes the new paper and holds it like a high wall between him and the family.

Amanda stands near the table in case she is needed. Because part of her duties is to be involved with the children, she tries to engage Edwin in quiet conversation, with little luck. She feels relieved when Sophie asks to be excused and grabs Amanda's hand, dragging her to the window.

"Where are we?" she asks loudly, looking out the window at the noisy station. They sit at the edge of a wide yard, and a few tracks away, another train has pulled in. People are stepping out with their luggage and walking away.

"This is a city called Chicago," Amanda explains. "We're in a train station. I'm not sure where exactly."

"Michigan Avenue," Mr. Evans grunts. No eye contact.

"You see there?" Amanda points. "Other trains can pull in. People are coming from all over the country. And other trains are leaving. It's a very busy place." The explanation goes on for some time as Amanda points out many things. Sophie seems interested in knowing more about the people outside the window. She asks questions and makes great guesses about what she sees. The woman in the large hat is probably going to California, she thinks. It will keep the sunshine out of her eyes. The man in the business suit is probably from New York. Then Sophie sees a family with a girl who is close to her own age. She knocks on the window and waves. The other girl looks surprised, but waves back.

Coaxing Sophie back to the breakfast table, Amanda heads toward the galley, just as Edwin rises to leave. He follows her out of the room

"I saw you get up last night," he mumbles to her in the tight walkway. "I saw you climb over to that mail car." She looks back at him blankly.

"There's a man staying in there, isn't there? I spotted him. He's been in there since we left New York. Do you know him?"

"I ... I don't know what you mean," Amanda stammers, immediately sorry that her response comes out sounding so flustered.

"Don't you?" The boy smiles slyly. He mouths something, but she can't quite make out the word. Then he brushes past her and heads back to his berth.

Amanda stays near the galley kitchen for the remainder of the morning, uncertain if she is in some sort of trouble. But the day continues on, and nothing more is said.

By midafternoon, the family has made its Chicago plans. They will not stay in the train cars for the rest of the week, and they will not need Amanda to come with them to the apartment. A spinster relative is visiting; she's made it clear to the family that she wants to dote on the children while they're here, and she isn't used to having servants around.

Amanda and the others are welcome to stay in the cars until the family returns, and they are given several chores to keep them busy. Once the family departs, she works at a feverish pace, finishing all her work in less than a day. This leaves her plenty of time to visit with Jeb, and maybe to see some of the city.

Jeb stops by to give her a smiling thank you for her previous night's visit, and to tell her he's moved out of the mail car, which has since been unloaded and hauled off for its return trip. Jeb has managed to secure living space for a couple days in two small rooms over the top of a garage located right behind the station. He wants to visit with her some more, he says, but that will have to be between his various meetings.

As Jeb walks away, Amanda continues to find herself fascinated by him. He did not come to Boston with a big network of friends, but he made some there and did all right. But it seems to be far different in Chicago. This is a powerful base for him. He found free accommodations quite quickly, and she knows he has several meetings. Many people seem to know and respect Jeb in this city. They take care of him.

They manage to meet up again late on the second day. As they stroll through the station, she hears whispers from the workers wherever they walk. People also stop to shake his hand. He seems to be a bit of a celebrity among workers and other people who have an interest in the labor movement.

They climb the stairs to the upper part of the garage, and Amanda finds that the front-most of Jeb's two rooms is set up with a table and chairs. He says he's been using the space to greet visitors and hold meetings. In the back, there is a double-wide cot. Jeb holds one more meeting, then he and Amanda spend the evening alone there, enjoying each other once again in quiet repose.

"I heard you and those men talking about Pullman this afternoon," Amanda says, her head resting on Jeb's shoulder as they lay naked beneath the sheets. "Why was that?"

"Oh, listening in on me were you?"

"Well, yes. It's kind of hard not to in this small space."

"So you know who Pullman is?" he asks, stroking her hair.

"I know the name of the company that makes train cars. I haven't ridden trains all that much, but I think half the cars I've seen so far had a Pullman logo on them."

"That's probably true, and that company is owned by George Pullman. It's his name, it's the name of the coaches he builds. And it's also the name of a whole town south of here."

"They named a town after him?"

"Not exactly. He built it and named it after himself."

Amanda props herself up on one elbow, toying with Jeb's chest hair. "Goodness. I can't imagine having that kind of money."

"Well, there's more to it than just that. It's sort of a workers' town, and I don't necessarily mean that in a good

155

way. We were talking about Pullman because I'm headed there tomorrow for a meeting."

"Such a busy man. I don't know how you keep all your various projects straight."

He traces his finger over her lips. "Will you come with me?"

"Out of the city?" She nibbles at his hand. "I can't."

"Why not? It's close by. It's only for the day. We'll be back by evening."

"I … I don't think I should. I'm new to my job and all."

"But you're all caught up, right? And the family won't be back for at least three more days. How would they even know?"

"You are such a temptation, Mr. Thomas." She kisses her way up his arm.

Jeb laughs. "As are you, Miss Grant."

Chapter 22

Parallel

"I would like your opinion on something, Victor, when you have a chance." Professor Alton leans over his lab table, heavy glass safety goggles loom over his tired eyes.

"Battery?" Victor laughed. "Another design?"

The professor nods. "Yes. And I suppose it's become my lot in life to be known as the man who builds prototypes, never a final product."

"Nothing wrong with that. Every technology starts with someone who follows a passion. Others get to build the products and make the money. You get to be the inventor. Just make sure you get your patents squared away."

After Professor Alton finishes soldering a connection, he lifts a box that's roughly the size of a liquor crate off his bench. He places it on the ground near Victor's feet.

"How many volts?"

"It can produce 17 for several minutes. Shake it a bit and you may get up to 20, but if you use it at that rate it will drain the battery much faster."

"Really? This is less than half the size of the last one I saw, and it's twice the voltage?"

"I've been busy Victor. Trying new chemicals. New mixtures. This is technically a dry cell. No more acid and lead. This one has nickel and cadmium electrodes embedded in a potassium hydroxide solution, but it's created as a paste. Nothing to spill."

Victor runs his hands over the metal box that contains the mixture. "Very impressive."

"Want to see it in action?"

"Of course I do."

Professor Alton has set up a series of lights along the top of his workbench. There are dozens of them. The wires feeding the lights run through a series of switches that allow the lights to be powered in two ways, either as a series circuit or a parallel circuit.

"First, let's do parallel." Reaching up, he flips all switches. The arrangement routes the power to the first six lightbulbs. They all glow at the same level, and the glow is fairly bright.

"Not bad. How long will it last?"

"Depends. It's not full max so the power could last a few hours. If I turned more switches and added more bulbs, I'd likely reduce the life of this charge by 10 minutes or so per bulb."

Victor nods. "Just being able to time it that precisely is progress. I remember your first batteries were hit or miss when it came to how long the power would last."

The professor smiles. "Just wait. There's more." He clicks the battery off, then adjusts his switches again. He turns most of them a quarter turn, resetting the circuit so the bulbs are now wired in series.

He turns the battery back on. "Now look."

As Victor expected, the bulbs glow again, but now each bulb is successively dimmer. Wired in series, bulbs do not get the same level of electricity if they are farther down the path.

Professor Alton holds up a finger, then reaches to his battery. He lifts a baffle, allowing more of each chemical to mix. All of the bulbs brighten a bit.

"Wow, that kicks out a lot of power,"

"Enhanced mode," the professor says. "Burns through the available power faster, but it's good for peak usage, if such a boost is needed."

He returns to his bench and flips more switches, adding more and more bulbs, until the full set of 12 are lit. Then Victor notices a set of wires on the end that extend to the far wall, where even more bulbs wait at the ready. As the professor flips the last switch an additional set of 12 light up. The lights definitely dim along the string, but with a little more fiddling with the battery's baffle, brightness is boosted greatly. Both men squint against the glow of the room.

As if to drive home the point that this is a better battery, the professor also attaches an electric fan to the end of the circuit. He fully opens the battery and they watch the show. In a couple of minutes, the full load starts to drain the available power. The lights dim. The fan slows.

"Very impressive, sir. Looks like you've addressed several issues, and in quite the compact package."

"Yes indeed. You know, Victor, it's funny. Batteries were the main source of electricity before we started building generators and setting up electrical grids. Every new type of battery used to fuel other advances, including the spread of telegraphs and telephones. But now, scientists like you are focusing on power plants and wires, instead of the lowly battery. But I still enjoy this work. The battery is portable. It unplugs you. You're free to wander with it."

"Well, like I said. It's impressive. Looks like you've made so many improvements, I'm not sure what it is you wanted to ask me!"

"Simple, my boy. I wanted to ask if you might want my previous version of this battery. It's only slightly larger. And I've already charged it."

Victor laughs. "Trying to corrupt me? Like you said, my work is in alternating current. Not DC batteries."

"Of course I understand that. But... does that mean your answer is no?"

Victor laughs, but says nothing

"Think of the fun you could have. The tests you could do."

Victor notices the other battery siting in the far corner of the lab. "I'm already thinking of that. Of course I want it. But I'm sure it's heavy. Can I borrow one of the college's hand carts?"

Chapter 23

Pullman

They prepare to leave just before dawn, as the first voices of weary travelers begin to fill the station.

Jeb has arranged for transportation on a beautiful, surprisingly long passenger train that sits five tracks over from where the Evans coach is parked. The locomotive is already steaming. A fireman arrived ninety minutes before the passengers, shoveling heavy scoops of coal into the furnace, tinkering with valves and gauges, and slowly bringing the massive front tank to a boil.

Amanda and Jeb first heard the rhythmic *tink tink* of the expanding metal as they awakened from their slumber. Dressed now, they enter the train yard. Even though they're still thirty feet away, he can feel the engine's heat as they approach.

As she and Jeb walk aboard, he guides her to a pair of seats in the first-class coach.

"Quite impressive!" she says.

"Isn't it? I may not sleep or eat in style, but once in a while I get to travel in luxury." He sighs for a bit. "You know, I haven't told you yet what our plans are beyond Chicago. This is probably a good time to do so. You realize, don't you, that I can't stay here for long? Nor can you."

She nods. "Of course I know that. You have work to do. And for now I go wherever the family goes."

"Well, I'm due in Kansas in two days. But I very much wanted to spend today with you. I'm glad you came with me. I hate that it won't be as long as I'd like. And I hate that I'll have to spend at least part of today working."

"And that's why I wanted to come with you to Pullman. And after what you told me of it, I guess I wanted to see it for myself." She looks at the crowded train and asks why so many people want to travel to the town of Pullman.

"Oh, usually this train only goes near or through Pullman on its way south. It normally doesn't stop there, but it will today. I've arranged to have us dropped." He winks. "After that, this train will continue heading south. She goes all the way to New Orleans."

Amanda smiles. "Now there's a place I've always wanted to visit."

"In fact," Jeb continues, "like a lot of trains, this one is named after its final destination—*New Orleans*. If you're heading south out of Chicago for any reason, chances are this is the train you'll have to take."

Amanda looks at the other passengers. She had hoped to see something exotic. If these people are heading south, shouldn't they look … well, southern? She's seen books and news photographs that show the huge Mississippi River and southern people. Those images showed striking, unusual faces, work clothes, and attitudes. They had a certain look to them that's hard to describe.

So why doesn't she see similar images here in this car, on these faces?

Something that's been lurking in the back of her mind suddenly comes to the front, like a bright light. These people, heading this morning out across the heartland then down south along the big river, all look prosperous and polite. She's wanted for so long to see the rest of America, the real country, and she's come to realize she's not going to see the real country. Not from a private train car. Not from a first-class coach. Not even from a home like the one owned by the Morgans.

Prosperous people, she's noticed, tend to have a certain look that makes them seem uniform in nature. If you were to stand a successful businessman from Chicago next to one from Boston or even New Orleans, they all would look only marginally different.

Bankers look like bankers. Lawyers look like lawyers. Whatever their ilk, businessmen and their wives wear their clothes and their attitude like military uniforms. Part of success seems to be looking like others in their tribe, especially as train travel has helped to blend one city into another.

The Greater Chicago area starts to look different as they roll southward. The brightness or dreariness of rich and poor neighborhoods that Amanda noticed on the way in seems muted now, especially since many of the streets stand empty at this early hour. Buildings are just buildings. The people inside are just people, equal in their need for sleep, peace, love, and family.

Her head rests softly on Jeb's arm, the two of them rocking in unison above the *click clack* of the heavy wheels and tracks. He slowly starts to nap, but not her. She wants to drink all of this in; even if the Midwestern landscape seems flat and dull, she wants to see it all. The trip, so far, has been a mix of wonder and intense stress for her. She wanted to perform well in her new job, to assure the Evans family that she's a good reliable worker. Now she finally has some time to relax. She's with Jeb, and the day is going to be grand. For the first time in months, she feels at peace. It's a wonderful sensation.

The trip to Pullman isn't a long one. A half hour into the ride, the conductor passes through the car quickly, collecting tickets and giving Amanda a sly wink as he moves past, never asking for hers.

"Five minutes," he says to Jeb.

Jeb stirs slowly awake while Amanda fixes her hair. They admire the sunrise for a while, and he asks her a few questions about her job.

"It's okay, actually. Better than I thought it would be. The family seems nice enough, even though I don't think I'll ever really get to know them."

"So how long do you think you'll stay with them?"

"I don't know. It's hard to say."

"Lifetime?"

She snorts. "Of course not."

"No, I can't see you doing that. You're too independent. This trip is just a bit of a lark for you, isn't it? A chance to try something new."

"It's a way to get back on my feet again, Jeb."

"Okay then … what *is* it that you'd like to do, long term?"

She smiles at him. "You know what? I've actually given that some thought. I think I might like to be a school teacher. I'm a good reader and fairly good at math. And I like kids."

"Yes, I can tell that you do."

"And I like inspiring people. Challenging them to learn, you know? Does that make sense?"

"Of course it does. I find you very challenging."

She frowns and he kisses her cheek. "I guess, too, that I want to be a mother. More than anything. A wife, a mother, a member of a community again."

"Lots of different ways to define 'community'," Jeb responds. "My community is out there."

Amanda looks out the window to see that they have reached the outskirts of Pullman. "What, right here?"

"Well, I'm not talking about any one place. I'm talking about the community of have-nots. I'm talking about honest, smart people who find themselves working, yet still in bad circumstances. If they're on the short end of the stick, I like helping them."

She nods. "I know you do."

"And I know that you'd be a good teacher," he says, "and a great mother, too."

"Thank you. And what about a good wife?"

He squints at her. "You know, I think you scare me a bit."

"Scare you? Why?"

"Maybe I was only half kidding when I said that you're challenging. You do like inspiring. You like pushing. You've said so yourself, and I've seen it. I've seen how you do it with me."

She doesn't say anything in response, which Jeb takes as reluctant agreement.

He pauses and then asks, "And how did your husband like that side of you?"

She stiffens a bit. "What do you mean?"

"You know what I mean."

"I don't."

The train starts to slow. The conductor passes through again, tapping Jeb on the shoulder. Jeb waits until he moves on.

"Okay, I guess I'll spell it out. I've been around enough union halls to meet hundreds of working men, and in the process I've also met their wives and families. You get to see certain types, you know? The ambitious man. The lazy man. The lazy man with the ambitious wife who nags him like she's riding a stubborn mule."

Amanda looks hurt. "And you think I'm that type of woman?"

"No, actually, I don't. With the right kind of man, I think you could be very inspirational to him. But with the wrong kind of man, I think he might not take to your inspiration. I don't think he'd accept it the way you intend it. He'd be threatened, mostly because he misinterprets it."

She turns away.

The train slows to a steady chug as it moves through the center of Pullman. Amanda, face pressed to the glass, is surprised by how busy the streets seem. She also has another reason to turn toward the window. She doesn't want Jeb to see her face at the moment.

He leans over, nestling against her back.

"You do know that you need to push. You push yourself all the time. You push the others who are around you."

"I don't like that word 'push.' It makes me sound nasty."

"Inspire? Help someone achieve their best? Be their muse? Do those words sound better to you?"

"Maybe."

Pullman looks much cleaner than Chicago. Crisp and new, it's like a toy town just pulled from its box. The place even smells new. The bricks are fresh and so is the wood.

The factory in the center of town sits snuggly against the houses without crowding them out of the way. The building includes a tall clock tower more appropriate for a school than a factory. The whole structure rises like a benevolent parent, and it watches, hawk-like, over the center of the village. Amanda sees workmen in neat gray overalls carrying wooden boxes as they navigate the sidewalks. A horse cart rolls by carrying what appears to be a load of glass train-car windows destined for the factory.

She sees so many workmen carrying so many different things; it seems as if the factory has spilled out onto the streets. Yet even with all this foot traffic, the streets seem clean and neat. Beautiful even. It really is a picture of a perfect town. Amanda feels intrigued immediately and reaches to hold Jeb's hand as they walk from the station.

"Disgusting, isn't it?" he says.

"What?" She thinks he must be joking. His reaction couldn't possibly be so different from hers.

"I ... actually I was thinking about how nice this town looks," she replies. "How neat and pretty."

"Well, yes," Jeb agrees. "I suppose it does look beautiful. Perfect streets. Stores conveniently located in each mini-neighborhood. Nice houses that are an ideal walking distance to factories. Men can even run home for a quick lunch if they want."

"Well, isn't that all pretty nice?"

"Normally, it would be great, Amanda. But this isn't a typical small town. Not at all. There's something more sinister going on here. Look closer."

She looks up and down the streets. "Sinister? I don't see anything bad at all."

"Just keep looking! Examine the whole place. So perfect that, well, how could it possibly be *this* perfect? No home looks better or worse than the others, does it? How about old people? Do you see any? I certainly don't! And do you see anyone who looks sick or crippled? I'm willing to bet you won't see one during our whole visit. And no drunks either. And let's not even talk about blacks or Chinese."

Amanda looks at the flow of workers. Jeb is right. She sees only two men with gray hair, and they're only slightly gray. Most of the people look healthy, hardworking, and very white.

"I don't understand," she admits. "What happens to the others? Every town has … well, all sorts of different people, including bums and the occasional crazy person."

"Oh, it's not like anything bad has happened to them. They haven't been removed. They were never here in the first place. This is strictly a workers town, Amanda. It's not a real town. There's over 4,000 acres of land here, and it all belongs to Pullman. The factory buildings were built right where Pullman wants them. The houses have been placed right where they will be most beneficial to the factory and its work. This whole damn town was built to keep workers happy and productive. It doesn't seem like a bad deal for them at first. Come to work here, and you get a place to live too."

"Really? Rent-free?"

"Well, no, not rent free. But at a decent discount. It's all arranged for you."

Amanda stops to look down a side street. The symmetry of all the buildings reminds her of a classic painting.

"Are you looking at it?" Jeb continues. "So many of the houses are exactly the same. Same brick. Same windows. Same doors."

"Yes. I can see that."

"Sidewalks? All the same. Front steps? All the same. Doorknobs and railings, too. All have been built from the same master plan. And that's just the beginning."

"So it's a planned town," Amanda says aloud.

"Yes. Planned around these specific jobs. Planned around the company."

Amanda tries to digest this. It's such a radical way of structuring a community that she doesn't even have an opinion about whether it's a bad thing or a good thing. It may seem sterile and strange, but no one looks unhappy.

"Well," she finally says, "I think it looks like a wonderful place to live."

Jeb shrugs. "Fair enough. But if the workers could own the houses," he gestures to a group of workers in the distance, "it might actually *be* a good deal for them. The town might seem more like a home. But these people can never own their houses. The company owns everything— houses, streets, and shops. They keep tight control, and that sort of control can be very calculating. Want a drink after a hard day of work? Tough luck. The only place that sells liquor is the lovely Florence Hotel. But the workers sure as hell can't afford to set foot inside."

Jeb urges Amanda to walk faster. He has meetings to attend. "This is the ultimate company town, dear. You can feel its looming presence everywhere."

"Yes, but if the company takes care of the workers ...."

"Well, that's the big word, isn't it? *If.*" Jeb waves his hands. "*If* is the big unaddressed issue here."

Amanda doesn't understand the politics of it. These people are thriving here. "Try to think of it the way I see it, Jeb. Compared to the struggles of farm life that I've seen, compared to growing up poor in the wrong part of a city, this doesn't look so bad to me. If I was living with no job in Chicago and if I thought I might end up out in the streets, I certainly would choose this instead. I know I would."

"Well, if the houses aren't theirs, then nothing really belongs to them here. Yes, they're comfortable for a while. But what if they lose their jobs? Back out into the street. No security. What if they get sick and can't work? Will Pullman take care of them? For how long? And if the company says to leave, they leave. They get no equity for the time they put in."

"Has he really kicked out sick people?"

"I don't know. I'm just talking theory. You have to understand how the labor movement views a place like this. But can you see what I mean? When a family lives here, their neighbors and friends are all employees. Their life, their families, their social existence, it all becomes so wrapped up in the company that they are totally at the company's mercy. If they argue, they could lose their home, job, and friendships. They can't afford to have everything they know come to an end. So they listen. They obey. They walk the line like ducklings because all the other ducklings are walking the line, too. Don't even think about squawking."

Jeb stops talking, realizing that he's been ranting like a preacher. "I'm sorry. I'll just put a cork in it now."

Amanda smiles. "It's all right. You're passionate about what you believe. There's nothing wrong with that."

Jeb excuses himself and ducks into the town's telegraph office, telling Amanda that he has a message waiting.

Amanda stays outside, admiring a large flower garden at the edge of a small green space.

Inside the office, Jeb speaks to the clerk at the counter. The man checks the general delivery shelf and hands him a yellow envelope. Jeb walks back toward the front window, using the light to read the telegram. It's a message from Boston, and it's not union business. The message is from Devlin Richards.

Before leaving Boston, Jeb had told Devlin to contact him via this office if there was trouble. Holding up the paper, he reads the handwritten scrawl, jotted down by the clerk as he listened to the click of the telegraph. Like many clerks, he noted when the telegraph stopped momentarily. It was a rough way of guessing where a sentence ended.

BOX IS TEMPORARILY INACCESSIBLE [STOP]

CHEN LU ALSO IN TROUBLE [STOP]

MAY NEED NEW PLAN WHEN YOU RETURN [STOP]

SOON? NEED TO VERIFY OUR ARRANGEMENTS [STOP]

PLEASE RESPOND [STOP]

-D.R.

Jeb folds the telegram and places it back in its envelope. He can see Amanda through the window, strands of hair curling around her face in the light breeze. A pang of guilt comes over him, but it quickly subsides as he tucks the paper into his pants. There's really nothing wrong with talking to Devlin, even though he stole the box from Amanda. It's just business. The girl, on the other hand, represents not business, but love. At least it might be.

Jeb takes a deep breath. Did he really just think that word?

He justifies his secret activities by telling himself that keeping track of the box is a way to eventually return it to her. And if there are riches inside, he'd surely share them with her. Maybe he could find a way to cut Devlin Richards and Chen Lu out of the deal, if there even is a deal. Risky yes, but isn't the woman standing outside the window worth it?

Jeb picks up a piece of scrap paper from the counter and writes a quick reply to hand to the telegraph attendant. He's deliberately vague.

WHY IS BOX INACCESSIBLE?

IS CHEN LU STILL AT HIS STORE?

WE'LL TALK WHEN I RETURN IN A FEW WEEKS

WOULD LIKE FUTURE UPDATES. WILL SEND FUTURE CONTACT INFORMATION WHEN AVAILABLE.

-JT

He pays for the telegram and walks out, picking up his conversation with Amanda right where they left off.

"You know, I'm not the only one who has problems with this town. A few years ago, a famous professor, Richard Ely, wrote a magazine article that said that power exercised by Otto von Bismarck in Prussia was 'utterly insignificant when compared with the ruling authority of the Pullman Palace Car Company' over this town. Isn't that great? I think that captures it perfectly."

Amanda raises her eyebrows.

"I've even talked to the minister in the local church," Jeb continues. "He compares life here to the old European serfdom system."

Amanda nods, slowly realizing that there could be personal risk in living in a place like Pullman. But part of her also wonders if risk isn't simply one of the prices of success. "You know, Jeb, except for some children, everyone I see here seems to be within about fifteen years of everyone else. While you were inside, I saw young mothers out walking their children. They were all together. In some ways, it's like a very special club here. It's like a fantasy place where everyone else is just like you. Almost like it was in grade school. I only wish I'd had something like this when I was married. Things might have turned out differently if Wayne and I had found this sort of support and community."

Jeb looks up at the clock tower. "But what if the community fails? It's great now, but Pullman can't keep growing forever. What if the demand for his coaches slows? What if some other factory finds a way to do it cheaper?

Will he have to cut the workforce or wages in a few years? If times get tough, will they drop the rent prices for all these nice houses? Or will they raise the rent instead? Do the workers get any say in the matter?"

Amanda doesn't have any answers.

"And where do they go to retire? They can't stay here. These are worker houses. If this is a real community, how does an old man stay near his friends and relatives when he's done with his job? Pullman doesn't care where you go, but you can't stay here!"

"My goodness, Jeb, is this our first argument?"

He smirks, more out of embarrassment than insolence. "No, no. I'm sorry to be ranting again. And I understand that it can be a good life for some. It's a real step up. And that's why Pullman has no trouble finding workers. But a company town is never a good thing."

They walk back toward the train station and look around for several minutes until Jeb finds his contact, a man named Fritz. They spot Fritz near the edge of the switch yard. He's a burly man with Navy tattoos on his forearms and morning whiskey on his breath. He keeps stealing glances at Amanda until she feels uneasy in his presence. Together, the three head toward the central coach car factory, Amanda trailing slightly behind. At the factory, Jeb will meet with a foreman who wants to form a local branch of the American Railway Union. They are all very secretive about the plan.

As they approach, Fritz nods slightly to a man near the factory's front walk. The man nods back and stubs out his cigarette.

"That man will get Silas. He's the one we're supposed to meet," Fritz tells them. "Silas will join us over at the market."

On their way to the market, which is attached to the side of the train station, Jeb explains that Silas could be immediately terminated if his supervisors knew of his union interest. "It's like a cancer to them. They'll cut out that cancer right quick if they suspect it's growing."

"Why does he want a union?" Amanda asks. She hears Fritz snort at the question.

"Why wouldn't he?" Jeb laughs. His takes on a condescending tone that unnerves Amanda. "For Christ's sake, no one's going to protect the workers but the workers themselves."

"That's for damn sure," Fritz grunts.

Amanda remains quiet while the two chat.

At the market they lurk around a fruit stand, and few minutes later a workman with neat hair and a bright mechanic's suit approaches them. He whispers to Fritz, then to Jeb.

"Can you excuse us, dear?" Jeb smiles at Amanda. "Business. Can we meet back here in, say, an hour?"

She nods, remains expressionless, and wanders out of the market.

Back out on the street, the midday sun prickles her neck. She seeks refuge inside a small millinery, attracted by a large yellow sun hat in the front bay window. She explores the long ribbons that flow off the back of the wonderful hat. Sitting in the shadow of the large hotel, this shop seems to be much fancier than the others in town.

A friendly shop girl invites her to try on the hat, in spite of Amanda's protests that she's only looking. They walk to a large wooden booth with two full-length mirrors along its sides, and a smile creeps over Amanda's face. The hat looks absolutely stunning on her. She's like one of the women in *Harper's* magazine, an urban sophisticate who knows things and does things that common women could never hope to encounter.

"That's amazing," the shop girl says. "You have the face and the figure, don't you? You should be a model."

Amanda smiles and tries on two more hats as a gentleman with a gray beard enters the shop. He asks the clerk for a certain type of ribbon, and she goes to the back room to find it. While she's gone, the man walks over to Amanda, coming to stand just outside the wooden booth.

"Who are you?" he demands.

Amanda stares back, perplexed.

"You're with them, aren't you? You're with that man."

She turns her back on him, but she can still see him in one of the tall mirrors.

"I know you hear me. Jeb's his name, isn't it? We know him, by God. You can bet your life we do. We don't know you, though …." He looks at her with menace. "But I guess I know your type."

Amanda decides her best tactic is to play the part of the lady she very much seems to be in her fancy hat, inside this fancy shop.

She looks the man up and down, defensively conjuring a look of disdain, which she wears like a shell. "I'm sorry, but we have not been properly introduced. I don't know you, and I think you are very forward, sir, coming up to me like this."

He looks exasperated. "Oh, do you now? Well, certainly you must be used to that sort of treatment, my dear. The man you are traveling with certainly is no gentleman."

She adjusts the ribbons on the hat. "Am I going to have to call a police officer?"

The man's face grows red. With his gray beard, he looks like a skinny St. Nicholas. "Oh, come now. And what would a policeman think? That I'm bothering a nice lady? We both know a proper lady would never travel with the likes of your friend. More likely you're some little plaything he picked up along the way. Go ahead. Call the police. We'd both be glad to run you out of town."

She considers slapping his face, but she holds back. She needs to know who he is, and how much trouble she might be in if she did so. Instead, she turns and walks back to the hat racks.

He follows and tries again to talk with her, but she continues to turn away. Finally the clerk returns from the back room, holding a fabric sample.

"Here we are. I think this is what you're looking for."

"Splendid!" he says. "But I was really hoping for something with a little blue stripe in it. It matches my wife's eyes, you know."

"Of course! I think we have something like that." The clerk hurries back to the rear of the store.

The man heads for the door, his voice rising. "You tell your friend to stay away from this town. Do you understand? Just stay away. We have ways of dealing with the likes of him. And his friends, too." As he reaches the door, he turns back, shaking a finger at her. "Neither of the men meeting with Jeb today will have a job tomorrow—I can tell you that much, my dear."

The door closes with a slam. Amanda is shaking when the clerk returns.

"I'm afraid the gentleman had to run," Amanda says. "A forgotten appointment, I believe." She looks at the clerk sympathetically. "And I shan't buy a hat today, either. But I did like that first sample of ribbon you showed him. Could I perhaps have three yards of that?"

When Amanda returns to the market, she tells Jeb of her confrontation. He looks troubled. Being outed as a unionist could put an end to some carefully crafted plans. The other two men are still nearby. Jeb talks to them for a moment.

"I may need your help," he tells her. "I'd like you to walk to the far end of the train station. Here, hold my coat and cap. I may need these and I may need them fast. The three of us are going to have a very public little confrontation over there. But don't worry. It's not real. At this point, I need to try to save these men's jobs, so don't believe everything you see and hear. I'll explain later."

She walks toward a distant door then turns, pretending to examine a rack of stereoscopic cards near a news counter. They contain scenes of things like the Chicago skyline, the Pullman factory, some Iowa cornfields, and small groups of Indians. Standing near the rack affords her a view down the length of the main hallway. At the other end, Jeb and the men start what looks to be a serious shoving match, with Silas shouting loudly. In less than a minute, two policemen and an older man in a suit come from opposite directions, drawn by the voices.

"You get your lousy stinking socialist union crap out of my factory and out of my town, you hear?" Silas shouts. "Just get out! I might have known that's what you were looking for when you asked to meet me!"

"I assure you ..." Jeb stammers.

"Let's get him!" Fritz yells, pushing Jeb again. They fall into a wrestling hold as the police arrive. The officers pull them apart roughly, with Fritz slapping the side of Jeb's head as they're separated.

"Here, here! What's the meaning of all this?" one of the cops demands.

"He's the problem!" Fritz shouts. "My cousin asked me to help get this man a job. He said he needed one, but now I find that it's a lie!"

Silas pipes up. "Yeah, Fritz arranged to have him meet with me because I'm looking for help in the shop. But then we find out he's not looking for a job. He's a stinking union organizer. The bastard!"

"Let me at him!" Fritz shouts. "Thought I was helping him. Play me for a fool, was that your plan? Couldn't get a meeting with us without lying?" He takes a step toward Jeb, his fist in a tight ball. The cop nudges them both aside.

"Look here, take it outside," one of the cops grunts. "And if you end up with fists flying out there, I'm arresting the whole lot of ya."

"I got no use for him. I don't want to see him again," says Silas loudly. "Get him out of here."

The police push Jeb toward the door. No arrest needed. But the man who arrived at the scene along with the cops—the man in the suit—beckons them. He whispers something in one of the policeman's ears. The cop reaches for his cuffs.

Jeb spins quickly, running down the hall toward Amanda. He seems to knock against her. But what he actually does is topple the card rack over into the path of the pursuing police. He also snatches his coat and hat out of her hands. In seconds he's out the door and around the corner. As he runs, he slips the coat and hat on like a rudimentary disguise. The police follow, but he has enough of a lead that they don't see his costume change. One more turn, and he's back alongside the train station again. He can hear the cops running away in the distance, assuming he's heading away from the building.

Cap thrust low over his brow, jacket zipped tightly, fresh cigarette dangling from his lips, he picks up a newspaper and looks like a different, totally relaxed man. He walks back into the station and over to help pick up the card rack. Then he motions to Amanda. They walk back toward the tracks and an idle train.

"What was that all about?" she whispers.

"Like I said, I had to help them save their jobs. They should be all right now. They'll look like heroes."

She takes him by the arm and can feel the tension coursing through him. The immediate threat is gone, as long as they don't run into the man with the gray beard again. He would definitely recognize Amanda, and probably Jeb, too.

"Damn!" Jeb sighs. "So much work just shot to hell. I can't believe I didn't know they were on to me. I never would have been so open about things if I knew someone was watching."

"Well, think of it this way," Amanda whispers, patting his arm, "you're famous around here. People know you and they're wary of your influence. Maybe you will be as big as Debs someday."

Once they reach the train platforms, his lips find hers. He's still a bit out of breath from running. In spite of her misgivings about what she's gotten herself into, she finds a sense of excitement when she's with Jeb. It's all a great adventure, and it brings a wild anticipation that she's lacked for so long. They lean against the back wall and kiss hungrily. They wait for Fritz's return. From a distance he will arrange their passage out of town. Jeb will head off to his other meetings. Amanda will return to her train-car family and eventually Chicago.

Chapter 24

Power Glide

Victor drags his new battery to the back yard of his rooming house. He's also procured a small electric motor that has a pencil-size drive shaft. It's capable of spinning a gear that's about the same size as the handle of a garden faucet.

He's already developed the foundation of an idea – one that will let him use this battery.

When looking through the technical manuals in Professor Alton's office, he noticed a paper that covered electric automobiles. There are no more than a handful of automobiles in the state of Massachusetts right now, and virtually none of them are electric. But they do exist. The paper described three such models, built in a variety of ways. Victor is also aware that the London Underground has used battery-powered electric cars from some short-distance runs.

The professor's battery is not as powerful as the ones needed to propel a heavy four-wheel vehicle. But its compact size makes it a potential power source for Victor's bicycle. He has had that idea in the back of his mind — almost since he first said yes and took possession of the bulky unit.

For the rest of the day, Victor makes several trips to a nearby hardware store and also a bicycle shop. First he adds a sturdy rack over the bike's back wheel to hold the boxy battery. Then he removes the back wheel and asks the bike shop to weld a second gear over the first. Back in his yard he needs to bend the bike's rear fork a bit to make it accommodate the now thicker sprocket. He does this by simply gripping each side and pulling. It's immensely satisfying to feel it bend to his will. He does feel bigger than ever. And stronger.

With a satisfied smile he turns his attention to the battery. It's easy enough to mount it to the bike rack. But actually using the electric motor proves trickier. He creates a shortened length of bicycle chain to connect the gear from the motor to the new gear he welded to the bike. Getting them to line up correctly takes nearly 90 minutes. But once everything is in place he bolts the parts down tight and wires the battery to the motor.

The wheel spins immediately. Victor realizes he forgot one important element. An off switch. With a little more cutting and wiring, he has he finished product – a bike that he can ride downhill like any other two-wheeler, but then he can flip on the motor to help push him back uphill.

He takes his Frankencycle out for a spin. With occasional stops to tweak this or tighten that, he eventually gets the machine running flawlessly. After four hills he feels the battery dying.

This so-called dry cell battery has an experimental element that makes it different from some other dry cells. With a little nickel and cadmium coating the electrodes and a bit of potassium hydroxide mixed into the paste, the battery can be recharged

Changing course, he heads over to Professor Alton's place, not only to show him his successful prototype powered bike, but also because it's the only place he knows that's set up to recharge a battery.

The professor is pleased and equally surprised when Victor unhooks the heavy battery and carries it inside.

"Look at you, my boy. Certainly looking much stronger and fitter than ever."

"That potion that your friend has been giving me seems to be doing wonders."

"Humm... yes. So I see. How much are you taking?"

"Not enough. Never enough. I'm loving this new me."

The professor raises an eyebrow, but says nothing.

They hook the battery up to the charger. It's a trickle of power and will take several hours to recharge. Victor looks impatient and angry. He doesn't want to wait. He's restless as he stares at the charging system. He taps his foot. Paces. Looks at his pocket watch.

To distract him, Professor Alton asks about the lens he gave to Victor.

Victor shows how he's attached the lens to his hat. "I don't need it all the time. But when my eyes get tired, you're right. It's nice to have. It corrects the drifting. Let's me work much longer, and I appreciate that.

At the professor's urging, they go across the street to a small restaurant to get some dinner. Back at the lab two hours later, Victor quickly unhooks the charged battery and reattaches it to his motor. With a quick wave, he powers off into the night. Professor Alton just looks after him, shaking his head. The young man seems to have as much energy in him as the newly charged battery. But it's a restless, angry energy that needs to be channeled.

Should he be worried about Victor? He's not sure. In some ways the young man is healthier than he's ever been, and certainly stronger. But this is uncharted territory, and Victor seems far too eager to plunge in without a roadmap.

Chapter 25

Alone

Glint of sunlight off dusty glass. A soft glow stretches out from a tall window, reaching across the raised platform just as Amanda's train pulls into Chicago. As she rolls past the window, she sees her own reflection for a split second. Then it's gone.

It's a quick trip from Pullman back to Chicago, but it seemed longer as she rode alone.

The sunlight falls over the left side of the train, causing many eyes to squint and heads to turn away. But the sun, having served its purpose, moves on and slowly fades. As the passengers disembark, the light has faded to a shallow red wraith, fragmented and bleeding on the tracks below.

Smell of stale beer and urine drifts over the platform.

Home. Such as it is these days.

She can see the Evans family train cars in the distance. Marta is visible through the windows, probably cooking a small meal just for herself and the butler.

Strange as it is to have a temporary home here in the middle of a train station, it still does feel good to arrive back at this base.

It's also good that the family is still away from the cars for a few days. She needs to relax. She also needs to ponder some of the things she heard Jeb say after their narrow escape from the Pullman police. She's not sure yet how to interpret his words.

As she walks down the platform toward the mansion on wheels, she wonders about Jeb. Where is he now? Was his train ride in the other direction a good one? How safe is he?

And, what has she gotten herself into, consorting with him? But in spite of any misgivings, his safety is a prime concern now. She needs to see him again, and talk to him.

Their departure from Pullman happened with surprising swiftness. Fritz, cursing their bad luck, arranged for Amanda to quickly climb onto a train that was headed back to Chicago.

Jeb had hurried off to another train, heading southwest toward his meeting in Kansas City.

"Why Kansas?" she asked. "What are you going to do there?"

Jeb mentioned something about the stockyards on the outskirts of the city, and the cattle cars, and the money being made by the men who moved both. The working men are entitled to some of that money, too, he boasted.

Amanda still doesn't understand the nuances of Jeb's business, but she does know that when money is being made, plenty of people seem willing to hire Jeb to help them organize and claim a piece of it.

Again on the return ride, she received little more than a nod from a conductor who never asked for her ticket. She slipped past, settling into a seat near the back of the last passenger car. Later, as the train idled just outside the town, taking on fresh water and bringing its boiler back up to steam again, that conductor, and another, actually joined her, much to her surprise. They settled into long seats that faced each other like a bench in a pub.

They introduced themselves. Both of them knew Jeb, and they wanted to meet her, too, since she appeared to be a good friend of his. It didn't take long before they started telling a few fond stories of Jeb and how he'd helped them a few times in recent years.

"He helped me get this job in the first place," one of them said. "Got my brother a job here, too."

"He helped me keep my job about six months ago," said the other. "They threatened to fire me when I had to take off two weeks. My wife was terribly sick. She had the flu something awful."

"How did Jeb help?"

"Came with me when I met with my supervisors. Had a book with him and he read the law out loud. Said they couldn't do what they were threatening to do. He made them mad as a wet cat, I'll tell ya, but they let me keep my job."

They also told of times he had surprised them and yes, on occasion, angered them, too. The stories went on for over a half hour.

The conductors nodded knowingly when she told them Jeb was on his way to Kansas City.

"I tell you, that town's already been a real hotbed of union activity. And fights? Oh my. I've heard some stories."

"What?" she asked. "What did you—"

"He's probably going to City Market," the heavyset one told her. "That's where the day laborers linger about when

190

they're looking for work. Not much more than tramps, some of them, but for a little pay they're willing to lend a hand for a day or two in the cattle yards or the butcher shops. It's a strange place. A real sense in that city that everything and everybody is temporary. Just passing through."

The thinner one, who possessed a slight Scottish accent, nodded. "Yeah. Some of the men in that business move between the Kansas and the Chicago yards. I've a cousin who's worked both places. He says it's real hit or miss with the work down there. Never knew how long it would last or what the pay would be. He finally got sick of it and came back to Chicago to work at the stockyards here. Least he's got family here. Says he's going to stay because it's steadier. Less crazy."

The heavy one leaned close to Amanda to deliver his next words in a hushed tone.

"I have to be honest with you, dear. I admire Jeb, and what he stands for, but he and his boys play rough sometimes."

Amanda frowns slightly. "What do you mean?"

"Leave it," the other conductor says to him. "It ain't your place."

"The devil it isn't!" the other shoots back, hand held up like a stop sign. "Either she knows all about him and is fine with it, or she doesn't. Either way, I think she should know. Am I right?"

"Bah," comes the reply.

Amanda leans closer so that she can hear what he says. "Look, dear, I'm not saying what he does is right or wrong. I think that part can be hard to judge. I'm just telling you what he does. That's all."

"A fine thing this is. I'll have no part in this," the thinner one says, and he stands and walks away, shaking his head.

Amanda watches him go, then leans closer to the remaining conductor. "Go on. Tell me what you mean," she whispers.

"Well, just that I think a woman needs to know what she's getting herself into. Might be that you already do, and if so, I apologize for being a fool and going on about it. And before I say any more, I also have to say that I think that man of yours is a fine man. I say he's a good man because he helps out the likes of me, and he helps us a lot. But it's a rough life that he's chose, and you got to be rough to live it."

"I know it can be. I've already seen a little of it."

"Well," the conductor continues, "Jeb's been arrested probably a dozen times or more, and not always for just promoting rallies and making speeches without a permit. Trouble is that Jeb, when he gets to running with some of the Debs crew, they take it up a notch. Vandalism. Assault. Even murder once, though he was never convicted for that."

"What?"

"Yes. Murder, dear. Just thought you should know. He claimed self-defense, and after a lot of court time, they finally believed him. He was lucky to get a judge that was sympathetic to the workers' cause. But it was a damn close one."

"What happened? I mean, how did it happen?"

"Happened right here in Chicago. Railroad bull didn't want him on railroad property. Picked Jeb up and threw him right off the land. But Jeb came right back. Lucky for him he had a piece of paper from the courts that said he had a right to hold a meeting. The bull just took it from him, ripped the paper up, and kicked him hard a few times right square, if you know what I mean. That might have been that, but the bull picked up a good old heavy stick and commenced to beating Jeb with that, too. Kept on beating him while he was lying on the ground."

"Oh my goodness."

"Yep. Nasty business, dear. Jeb had a gun in his boot. He just reached in, aimed right up, and shot that railroad cop through the chest."

Amanda shivers. From the way the conductor describes it, it seems to be a clear case of self-defense. But still, hearing that someone she knows so intimately has killed another person is harsh.

"Well, I can see why he wasn't convicted," she says. "It's a terrible thing, but … I guess … a man has a right …."

"Yes, he does. If it was just open-and-shut self-defense, it might never have even gone to trial. But then some additional facts came to light. I guess Jeb and that particular guard had some run-ins a few times before. Some said Jeb even set up the whole incident, making sure he had the paper and everything, as a way of prompting a fight and getting revenge. Then there's the question of whether he should have warned his attacker to back off before shooting him. Could be the bull never saw the gun. A lot of gray area there. Enough so that the police charged him. Luckily for him, he successfully pleaded his case and got off."

"I see."

"Do you? I wonder if you really do, my dear." They sit in silence for several moments.

"Well, anyway, I've said enough. Not even sure why I've told you all this. Like I said, I really do think Jeb's a good man, and I'm glad to have him on my side. I just think a woman needs to know what she's getting herself into."

And that was that. The conductor went back to his rounds, and she soon found herself back in Chicago.

Now here she is, returning to the Evans cars, thoughts swirling. Jeb travels in a world that's much more complex than the business world she had pictured. Where she sees opportunity, he interprets oppression. Where she sees growth, he sees exploitation. His arguments always make sense if she listens to them long enough. She feels naïve around him. He knows so much, and she seems to know so little.

She reaches the cars but doesn't climb on board. She just leans against the side. How honest is Jeb, really? Even if his cause is just, is he overcommitted to his ideals—to the point of treachery? Are there other women? He visits so many cities. He so often travels alone.

As she climbs up into the second of the two ornate cars, Amanda detects something wrong almost immediately. There are glances from the cook and the butler, but no friendly smiles. Her greetings are returned with polite nods. Her questions receive one-word replies. There is no eye contact nor intimacy of voice.

"So," the cook says, "Mrs. Evans, Edwin, and Sophie came back today."

"But I thought—"

"Yes, the family is still staying the whole week. But they were on a sightseeing trip, and they came back to gather some things. And, well, they also came back to talk to you."

Amanda looks at her feet. She doesn't like where this is leading.

"Mrs. Evans and the children are sitting in the front car," Marta says. "She asked that you immediately pay them a visit upon your return."

Amanda nods, swallows hard, and walks through the dining area, past the button-tufted chairs, and into the main sitting room.

Edwin is sprawled casually across a plush davenport. His lackadaisical attitude alarms her. He would never sit like that unless his mother wasn't distracted by other matters.

Mrs. Evan herself sits in a rounded-back chair that's upholstered over every inch of its surface. She looks like a queen upon a padded throne. Amanda suspects she would look equally at place behind a desk, running a large company, and she wonders how much of her husband's success can be traced right back to Mrs. Evans' influence.

Amanda smiles politely.

The only returned smile comes from Edwin. But it seems more of a smug grin. He doesn't look shyly away this time when she intently returns his gaze. He stares right back at her.

There is a quiet stirring in the back of the second car, near where Mr. Evans keeps a small office. The door is closed and Sophie is nowhere to be seen.

"Sit down, dear." She nods toward one of the chairs directly across from her. Amanda does so. She continues to look toward Mrs. Evans, but finds herself focusing on the wall behind the woman. She can't quite bring herself to look her in the eyes.

"I've heard some things that trouble me, dear. Is there anything you'd like to tell me?"

Amanda shakes her head no, not sure what she means.

"The man you have been seeing. You know of whom I speak. His name is Jeb, no?"

"I … I'm not sure what you mean by 'seeing,' ma'am. But yes, I have a friend named Jeb."

"He's poison, dear, and from what I hear, apparently he has poisoned you."

Amanda finally looks directly at her, silent. Confused. She notices how much taller the overstuffed chair is than hers. She suspects Mrs. Evans chose it on purpose, to increase her appearance of authority.

"Excuse me, ma'am?" She isn't sure why she's suddenly started to use the word ma'am.

"You know what I mean."

"No, ma'am. I'm afraid I don't."

The older woman squints. "Well then, why don't I spell it out for you? First of all, our family business is already having trouble with unions. Theirs is not a cause that we ever will support. Second, I try to make sure my family is exposed to good, proper values at all times. I'm afraid that you have created a small problem for us."

"Oh? How so?"

The older woman sighs. "If I must be specific, Edwin tells me that you visited a mail car. It was the one linked to ours during the trip. He said you stayed in there much of the night. Later I've found out that this beau of yours, this man named Jeb, was traveling in that car."

Amanda elects to remain quiet. But she does not look away. She looks right at Mrs. Evans and listens intently.

"Surely you can see the problem, dear. An unmarried couple behaving like that. And in front of my children. Why, I should have you arrested. You know there are laws against adultery. The problem is, I'm not quite sure which state we were in when you committed your crime."

Mrs. Evens looks Amanda up and down. This time she's the one who breaks off the eye contact.

"I trusted you, my dear. I brought you into what is essentially my home on the road, and this is how I'm repaid? With the most tawdry of indiscretions? A *mockery.* That's what it is. If that's what I wanted my son to witness,

I might as well have booked him a ticket on a carnival train!"

They both sit in silence. Finally Amanda gathers the courage to speak.

"I'm sorry, ma'am. You're right. It was not the time or place for that, and it was wrong of me to visit that other car." She gulps and waits, then adds, "He is a friend. I was glad to find that he was nearby, and I very much needed to see him. To talk with him. But I understand your concern, and if you want me to leave, I understand."

Mrs. Evans nods. "I do indeed want you to leave. But not for the reason of your tasteless little visit, dear." She sends a grumbling Edwin to join his sister back in the study. He sticks his tongue out at Amanda as he departs.

Then Mrs. Evans leans over the desk, confiding in her soon-to-be former maid and nanny. "If it makes a difference, I should tell you that I don't think you are a trollop. I don't see that in you. I am aware of your hard time in your marriage, and aware that a woman has needs. Any woman has a desire for romance. It can be quite difficult to find a proper chaperone while traveling. Also, I fear that what has happened is that you fell under a spell of a man who, frankly, has a reputation as a bit of a lothario, from what I hear."

Amanda looks at her, half in anger, half determined to see the conversation through to find out what message the woman is hoping to deliver.

"Yes, my dear," Mrs. Evans continues. "There is a lot that you don't know about your friend."

"It seems that I'm finding out more all the time. I'm interested, though, in how you know so much about him."

"I've never met the man. I was simply told about him by someone who saw him come out of the mail car. Someone at this station who knows a great deal about his union activities. And here's the gist of it. Perhaps you already suspect that you are far from his only beauty. He ingratiates himself quickly." Mrs. Evens squints, then whispers slowly, judging the weight of each word. "But the main thing, for me, is the business that he conducts. That is the main reason why my contact told me of his presence. It's the reason why I am so upset. You know what that is, no?"

"I do. Like we said, he works with the unions. He's a labor organizer."

Mrs. Evans raises an eyebrow. "You work for us. Lived with us. I'm sure you know our feelings about such things. And if you don't, you should. The union threatens my husband's business interests. It threatens our family and it threatens the very status of us all. And yet you continued in his acquaintance. Became his friend. Apparently his lover, too."

Amanda looks the older women in the eye. "Yes. Apparently ...," she smiles.

For the first time, she sees her employer look flustered.

"Yes, um ... well, my dear, I'm afraid your employment here is over. I'm not going to just cut you loose in a strange town. I'm happy to give you a ticket back to Boston or to any other place you'd like. Consider that your severance package, and it's more than you deserve."

Amanda thinks about this for a moment. "A ticket to Kansas City would be fine."

Mrs. Evans laughs. "Are you kidding? That's a rough-and-tumble place, my dear, and I know from good authority that's where your friend Jeb just went. Why on earth would you want to meet back up with a rogue like that, especially there?"

Amanda smiles. "You let me worry about that. And I do appreciate the ticket."

Amanda stands to leave, then turns back when she hears Mrs. Evans mutter "foolish girl" under her breath.

"I think you've misjudged me, ma'am. Do you think Jeb is foolish also? For getting involved with me?"

The woman laughs. "Of course not. You're young, pretty, and smart. What man wouldn't be attracted?"

"Then perhaps I'm not foolish at all, and perhaps things are going better than you realize." She winks at her and walks away.

She is allowed to stay in her bunk only for the night. She agrees to leave first thing in the morning. A train to Kansas City departs at daybreak.

Later that evening, Amanda passes the smirking Edwin in the car's narrow hallway. When he shoves his way past her, she whispers in his ear as he walks by, "Perhaps you're lucky that I'll be gone, boy. You might have had a hard time if I'd stayed. You would have had to learn some manners."

She can almost feel his face drop as she walks away. She can almost hear the eyes blink behind her. Then she adds, "But someone will likely teach you that lesson soon. Mark my words."

When morning breaks, she is out of the car in less than five minutes, clothes gathered and tied in an old tablecloth.

The first thing she discovers is that the train to Kansas City is having some engine trouble. It will be delayed about three hours. She spends the time sitting quietly on a lobby bench, reading and looking at the police officers who mill about the hall. They have no idea who she is, or what her history is with the police officers down in the town of Pullman.

She smiles with a certain satisfaction. Rather than being worried about losing her job, she starts to look forward to her next adventure with a good deal of confidence. She's a survivor. She knows that now. No matter how bad things get, she can survive.

She starts to think about how exciting it will be to reach the Missouri River and the mushrooming city that rests along its banks between Missouri and Kansas. It will be the farthest west—and the farthest away from home—she has ever traveled in her life.

Chapter 26

Short Sharp Shock

Victor Marius is flying.

He's glad he swapped out the gears on his bike, bolting on the larger mechanism. The difference ratio makes the uphill climbs on his electric bike a bit more battery-draining. But on the downhill side? It even accelerates there – after he's reached the previous limits of his coasting speed.

The difference is daunting, dangerous, and intoxicating.

Donning a pair of modified safety goggles against the wind, fat leather top hat crushed down against his head, he cruises around town like a man possessed, spooking horses and prompting curious children to run after him.

But can he do better? Go faster? What else can he tweak? The only problem he's encountered is that the bumps sometimes shake loose the nuts that lock down the wires. He's started carrying a pair of insulated rubber gloves so that he can make adjustments to the wires without having to turn off the power.

Today he's on his second trip through downtown Boston. Eventually he stops at Professor Alton's to leave the battery for a recharge, and he uses that time to look for work.

Victor remains interested in finding employment either at a power station or on the wire crews that string copper wires along telephone poles. Either one of those positions seem like good honest work, and that's all he wants to tackle at the moment.

Back on his bike for the afternoon, he rockets once again around Boston Common, then heads over to the train station. Coming around a corner near the far end of the yard, he feels the bike skip and lose power. It's a tell-tale sign the wires are coming loose again.

Pulling over to a space near the tracks, he steps off to make an adjustment. It takes him a few moments to notice there are hobos nearby, gathered near where the trains exit the yard. Some hope to hop aboard, while others are content just to stay in the shade, watching the cars pass.

For the most part, hobos are harmless. But there are occasional desperate ones, and Victor knows, by the look of the one walking toward him right now, that desperation can lead to aggression and clouded judgment.

"What'ch got there?" the hobo demands. He walks with a swagger and speaks with a tone of voice that seems predatory.

"You know what it is. It's a fucking bike," Victor replies, opting to show no nervousness to the man's aggressions.

"I know it's a fucking bike. What's with the other things? The big box. The wires. All that."

"Experiment," Victor replies. "Electric bike."

"That so. Well I'll be. Bet that's worth some money, eh?"

"Wouldn't rightly know. Never seen one bought or sold."

As Victor works on the loose connections, the hobo puts his hands on the bike. "Well ain't this nice."

Rather than reattaching the wires, Victor suddenly has a different idea. He leaves the battery ends connected but disconnects the wires from the motor. He takes the exposed copper ends of the wires and wraps them around his rubber-gloved fingers, one near the base of his index finger and one near the base of his ring finger.

"I think maybe you took a wrong turn, hum bicycle boy?"

"No," Victor replies, "I'm pretty sure I'm exactly where I wanted to be. Thanks for asking though."

The man tightens his grip on the bike. "I think you misunderstand me. You took a wrong turn. You leave now, and you leave this bike with me. That's our fee for you trespassing on this here property where we have our camp."

"Yeah… I don't think that's going to happen." Victor can feel a rage well up inside of him. It's both familiar and strangely foreign.

Familiar because it's like a switch that turns on in a moment of panic. The surge of desperation actually is what helped him fight and claw his way out of the Gossamer as it sank.

But also foreign because now it seems strangely amplified. It's as if the same thing that's helped him recover his muscle mass has also lit a fire in him that can easily flair up high and out of control.

The hobo doesn't know what he's asking. It's dangerous. It's….

The disheveled man tries to yank the bike away from Victor. That's all it takes to set Victor off. He swings and punches hard. Not only is it a good heavy swing and a well-landed blow, he hits the hobo square in the chin right where the wires are wrapped around his knuckles. The man's face dutifully connects the circuit as Victor's fist makes contact. A spark jumps.

Victor isn't sure if it's the jolt from the battery or his good punch, but the man goes down hard. He tries to drag himself back up, but Victor leans forward and punches again. Then he holds the wires in place for several seconds, seeing the man twitch. When he pulls his arm back he sees two half-inch lines of burned flesh on the hobo's chin. There's also a little burned rubber there from Victor's glove.

Victor steps back and looks at the other hobos standing in a line near some trees. "Anyone else?"

They look away. One man goes back to what he was doing—puffing opium from a stout pipe.

Victor looks down at his hand and sees that the wires have burned through the rubber. It's only then that he feels the pain of the burn. He's hurt himself a little in the process of fighting the other guy.

Peeling away the wires and then the rubber, he sees tender loops burned around each finger. Not terrible, but painful.

"God damn it," he exclaims as he licks the burns.

"That there was quite the punch," says the man with the opium pipe. "But now your fist, it hurts, too, no?"

"Yeah. Guess so. Do you know this asshole?"

"Maybe a bit. We call him Rumor. Always telling tales. Always hassling someone and saying it's their own fault for getting hassled. None of us really like him. Got to say, it was good to see him get punched."

Victor laughs. "Glad I could do my part."

The man offers Victor a puff of his pipe.

"No thanks. That stuff isn't for me,"

"Try it. It will make those fingers feel better. Or at least you won't care."

Victor chuckles. But… his fingers do hurt. Quite a bit.

"Well, maybe…"

It turns out that the opium does make fingers feel better. And it makes for a hell of an interesting ride home.

Chapter 27

Station

The morning rain is light enough that Jonathan Morgan decides to keep his scheduled long walk over to a neighborhood police station. It's a squat brick building located a few blocks from Chen Lu's shop. Jonathan has to walk past that shop on his way, so he stops to peer inside. The big main room is nearly empty. A handwritten "CLOSED" sign hangs in the front window.

Arriving at the station, he tries to ask some questions, but the officer on front-desk duty is more interested in writing in his duty log. After a brief protest, the officer agrees to check his records. Eventually he confirms there was indeed a police report filed about a burglary at the Jonathan Morgan home, so with further prodding he is escorted to a room near the back of the building, tucked between a set of jail cells.

Jonathan finds the room piled high with antiques of many styles. Most appear to have been removed from Chen Lu's shop. He is not allowed to touch anything, but he is allowed to look at the collection to see if he recognizes the box that was stolen from his home.

Items are piled on top of items and others stacked under the tables. He cranes his neck to and fro and bends down in order to see as much as he can.

"No," he finally says. "I don't see it."

"Well, that shop owner bought and sold a lot of things. Even if he did have it, it could be long gone by now."

"What did you do with him?" Jonathan asks.

"He's locked up in one of our cells. He won't see the judge for a few days, and he's not going anywhere until he does."

Jonathan thanks the policeman for his time and apologizes for being so insistent. As he nears the front door, the officer calls after him.

"Look, sorry I gave you a hard time earlier. We've been incredibly busy."

Jonathan nods.

"You know," the cop continues, "there are a couple other things we could check. We just haven't been able to yet."

Jonathan is about to put his hat on, but he pauses and asks, "Other things? What sort of things?"

"We found some safes in the back room of the shop. Two or three of them were locked. The old guy hasn't been very cooperative about helping us open them, so we're going to have them drilled out."

"I see."

"Tell you what. You come back here in a few days, and I'll tell you if we found any kind of box inside. You know, like the one you described. Okay?"

"And if you do? Will you release it to me?"

"Are you listed with us as the owner?"

"Well, technically no. But it was stolen from my house."

The duty officer shakes his head. "I'm only supposed to release it to the owner."

"She's moved," Jonathan explains. "I don't know where."

The policeman shrugs.

"Well, either way, I'd like to know if the box turns up. And if it does, I may try to track down the owner, though I'm not sure where she went."

"If you do, she can file paperwork to get it back. She just needs to prove that it belonged to her in the first place."

"Oh," Jonathan frowns. "Well, how does she do that?"

The cop snorts. "She ought to know that, shouldn't she? Tell her to collect all the necessary information, maybe tell us what's inside, and have her file her claim. Best I can offer."

Jonathan nods at the policeman and heads home, not at all sure the box will ever turn up, or that he'll ever hear from Amanda again.

Chapter 28

More

Life has become intoxicating to Victor Marius. The very act of being alive, of feeling every sinew and connection in his body, that's what draws him in. That's what makes him feel human, connected and thriving.

Every muscle seems to swell and grow, while also seeming to whisper their thanks to him for making it all happen. This is a new way of life for him and he drinks it in with gusto.

For the last several days he's risen before the sun. Out in the backyard he lifts his homemade barbell with the heavy brass gears. Fifteen repetitions. Thirty. Forty-five. His endurance grows.

Then push-ups. Sit-ups. Then a long run, with the intention of warming down, but he ends up pushing himself father than he's ever run before.

Yes, he works especially hard after receiving a shot of Dr. David Burke's magic elixir.

His run takes him past the train yard, and he spies the bully known as Rumor. But this time the man wanders off and keeps his distance.

He also sees the hobo who offered him a puff of his opium pipe. That man nods hello, and Victor stops to talk with him.

The opium actually did help his burn feel better, and Victor tells him so. Could it do the same for sore muscles?

The hobo nods. "Good for everything, this pipe is. Good to sooth. Good to blur the lines."

Victor has a few dollars in his pocket, and he makes a small purchase. It's against his better judgment. He's heard all of the terrible stories about what opium can do. But he's too smart for that. He knows he is. This is just a temporary thing, while he's working to get back into shape.

It's just… another experiment.

Chapter 29

Twain

The ride toward western Missouri goes on and on. Never has Amanda seen a flatter landscape. It's like traveling across an infinite plane, void of anything but the occasional farmhouse and cornfield. In between there is grass. And wheat fields. Even this early in the summer, everything seems grayish brown. Or maybe that's just her mood – because she hoped the trip would be more interesting. She looks to the horizon, anticipating the arrival of anything different at all as the train rolls on. Perhaps it might be a tree, another farm, a cow. What else could there be out here?

She wants to see something that will bring a slight sense of anticipation and wonder. The most she sees are some small patches of woods far off in the distance and a plowman or two working their fields. What must that be like, to till a field that has no end? How can they do that hour after hour? What occupies a person's mind when they are out there all alone, hours of work behind them and hours more ahead?

The thoughts in Amanda's head merge with the *click-clack, click-clack, click-clack* of the train wheels.

Same thing, same thing, click clack. Mile after mile.

A town comes and goes, the train whistles as it approaches, but no one waits at the tiny station. The locomotive barely slows, then chugs on. Amanda notices an empty wine bottle near the tracks as they pull away.

Two miles later, she sees a boy with a fishing pole walking near the tracks. He turns and waves at the train. He doesn't really smile. She studies the boy's face. Can the sun and the wind in a place like this change a person, too? It seems to take the color from people's cheeks, leaving them as gray as the sky.

On most trains, conductors collect the books and periodicals left behind by the riders. They stack them in a rack, often near the train's dining car, if it has one. Amanda decides to take a stroll down the aisle, to stretch her legs and to look for something to read. She particularly wants to find something that will tell her more about the part of the country where she is traveling. Looking out the window may be giving her the wrong impression of the place.

Amanda finds about three dozen books on a wire shelf. A thin rope stretches across the books to keep them in place. Scanning the titles on the spines, she selects a tattered copy of *Life on the Mississippi* by Mark Twain.

She doesn't know much about Twain, but she has read a couple of his magazine articles. She does remember he's from Missouri. Since she's heading there, this seems like a good choice.

It's always been fascinating to Amanda that America's eastern, southern, and then western sections were settled first, while the immense central area of the nation still stood relatively empty, except along its big rivers.

She opens the book and reads slowly, hoping Twain's words will offer some insight. She reads:

When I, as a boy, first saw the mouth of the Missouri River, it was twenty-two or twenty-three miles above St. Louis, according to the estimate of pilots; the wear and tear of the banks has moved it down eight miles since then; and the pilots say that within five years the river will cut through and move the mouth down five miles more, which will bring it within ten miles of St. Louis.

Amanda wonders at this prediction, then looks at when the book was printed. It's already more than five years old. Did the river indeed migrate? Do things really change so quickly in these parts?

She has heard about the wild floods that occur on the grand waterways. The Mississippi in particular has a tendency to spill its banks and redraw its curves every few years. How do people survive in a place where the acres just roll on and on, where rivers change their course, and where landscape changes so quickly?

They survive because they have to. Just as the first settlers in New England survived in the early 1600s. Just as she is surviving now.

She returns to her seat with the book.

A few hours later the train finally pulls alongside the huge Missouri River on its way into Kansas City. Amanda watches in wonder. The endless dead gray of the plains gives way to a colorful pulse of community and commerce. It's the first time she's had a real-life glimpse of lumbering, three-story-high paddleboats. There's also a sprinkling of smaller barges and rafts. It's like she's in a whole other country.

She sees two black men drifting in a flat-bottom skiff. One of them raises a string of catfish and shakes it for the train, laughing when the engineer responds with a quick toot of the whistle.

One of the hulking paddleboats hears the whistle and responds with a long, low blast of its own. The noise echoes off the low hills.

Kansas City appears in the distance. Amanda realizes that she's reached the very heart of the country. As they near the train station, she sees building after building. All of it seems new. New brick, new stone, new wood.

"Have you ever been here before?" asks a woman seated across the aisle.

"No. Never," Amanda replies.

"I grew up near here, but I've lived in Chicago for the past five years. It's good to come back for a visit."

"I never realized how wide the river is," Amanda remarks. "I can't imagine what it must have been like for explorers to see it for the first time."

"When we were coming into the city, did you see that tall hill?" the woman asks.

"I don't remember. I guess I probably did."

"Well, when the Lewis and Clark Expedition first arrived here, ready to explore the new territory, they camped on those bluffs overlooking the Missouri River. That's the first written record we have about these parts. One of them wrote in his diary that the site would be an ideal location for a trading post. And that's how this city got started, you know. It was just a trading post."

Amanda smiles. "And how do you know all of this?"

"Why, I'm a teacher! Off for the summer and coming back to visit my folks."

"I don't know much at all about this part of the country," Amanda admits. She holds up the book that she's been reading. "But I'm trying to learn."

For the next several minutes as the train slows and chugs through the outskirts of Kansas City and into the station, the teacher bends Amanda's ear about Missouri, the northeast corner of Kansas, and the wide river that separates the two.

Chapter 30

Undercurrents

Just before sunup Victor rides his electric bike to the train station in Boston. He hides it in the bushes near the back of the train yard and boards the first train he can find that's headed to New York City.

He arrives by late morning.

Rush of footsteps down a brownstone staircase.

Friendly greetings. Handshakes by the curb.

He finds his mentor, Nikola Tesla, just as the engineer is heading out, coat draped over his arm and hat perched perilously askew on his head.

"Delightful to see you, Victor. Yes, indeed. Absolutely delightful!" As is his custom, Tesla does not extend his arm for a handshake. Just one of his many quirks.

"And you, too, Nikola."

"Unfortunately I didn't expect you until tomorrow morning at the soonest. I'm on my way out now, with plans to attend a late-evening lecture at Columbia College."

Tesla explains that the lecture will focus on the two competing types of electricity, AC and DC currents. "Say, do come with me!" the engineer insists. "This talk is being given by the notorious Professor Herald Brown!"

"What?" Victor is visibly shocked. "I wouldn't ever want to see that man speak! Why would you waste your time?"

"Why? Well, why not? Don't you like to know what the competition is up to, lad? Don't you want to hear his latest claims and lies?"

Victor shakes his head. "No. Not that charlatan. He's such a strong advocate of DC current I'm surprised he doesn't have wires coming out of his head. He's a bit of a showman too, eh?"

"That's what I'm counting on, Victor!"

After they chat for a bit, the inventor manages to convince Victor to accompany him and also invites him to grab a quick supper first at a pub on Mulberry Street. After their meal they catch a northbound horse-drawn streetcar.

Victor jumps up into the car first, then grasps Tesla's arm and pulls him up quickly, almost effortlessly.

"Well, my boy, at least you have your strength back!"

"I've been exercising like a demon my friend. I had to. Now I find that it's helped a great deal."

Settling in near the front seat, they ride to 49th Street and Madison Avenue. Columbia College has stood near that spot, sprawled across several buildings, since 1849.

Victor tells Tesla everything as they ride, of both successes and failures, and of shipwrecks and fires. Tesla listens with grim concern. He has been very interested in Victor's tests and is troubled by the turn of events.

"I can't tell you how disappointed I was, Victor, when I heard that you and all of that wonderful equipment had been lost, even before your new set of experiments could be conducted. It's a pity. A pity, indeed."

"Might have been better if they saved the equipment and not me," Victor laments. "That could be more useful than I am at this point."

"Science marches on, my boy. And I wish they had saved both."

Tesla offers his sincere condolences for everything Victor has been through, including the wreck, the loss of his lab, and his current lack of employment. "Something will turn up, lad. You know it will. The world needs men of your talent right now."

Victor looks out the front window of the trolley, at the backside of the massive plow horse as it pulls the car uphill. He remains silent for a while, preferring to just listen to the echoing *clop, clop, clop* as the horse progresses.

"If you say so, Nikola. I don't feel nearly so positive about my future right now."

"Nonsense. Maybe you can't do research right now, but you are still very employable. I'm sure you could walk into any of the new electrical companies sprouting up back in Boston. Most of them would hire you in a minute."

"Maybe." Victor leans back against the wooden bench, staring this time at the trolley's ceiling. "Speaking of electricity, tell me why you want to go see this man tonight."

"Who, Brown? His lecture? Bah ... it's not that I *want* to see him. It's more that I want to hear some of the outlandish things he claims. You know very well that he's the man who's most responsible for our bad publicity these days."

"Meaning you and your ideas, and maybe Westinghouse's, too?"

"Meaning all of that. Yes." Tesla nods. "I consider this more of a spy mission than an opportunity to hear a worthwhile lecture. If I don't respect his views and his science, I sure as hell am not going to learn anything new from what he has to say."

"Really? You're mostly going to spy?"

"Yes. I hate giving him the honor of our presence. But we very much need to keep an eye on him right now."

"Why?" Victor asks. He looks out the window and sees they're approaching the edge of the Columbia campus.

"The man is big trouble for us." Tesla's Croatian accent grows thicker and heavier when he's angry. "He just … he just makes me …." Victor holds up a hand, trying to slow him down.

"It's not just because I consider his knowledge of electricity barbaric," Tesla continues, undeterred. "It's because he's been actively campaigning against all that we represent. I have developed—*we* have developed—a superior solution. What's worse, this Professor Brown seems to have gathered many admirers lately. The newspapers seem to love his dire warnings and circus-like performances. That could ruin me. It could ruin you, too, you know."

Victor shrugs. "I'm already ruined, Nikola. Being ruined by Professor Harold Brown might actually be a step up for me."

Tesla looks irritated. "Oh, stop feeling sorry for yourself, lad. You have many opportunities open to you if you just look for them." He looks around and suddenly laughs. "Why, let's start with this streetcar, Victor. Drawn by a horse! Today, it can be done with electricity. They already have them in New Jersey. You know it's the future of these buckets and so does our dear Professor Brown. And you know what? There's an opportunity for you right there. Only AC current will work efficiently over the distances traveled by electric trolleys. The challenge for us is that people like Professor Brown hope to ruin that. They'll delay our progress by ten years if they have their way. Maybe more. And they'll try to sell as many cities as they can on the idea of small DC substations strewn around every neighborhood. It's madness, simply madness. But Edison's a powerful salesman and so is Brown, his lackey."

Victor shrugs, but Tesla has already stepped down. "I know I've seen his name in the papers again within the last several months."

"Oh, you've seen him in print, all right," Tesla responds, "and I can tell you where. Big story about a year ago. Does the name William Kemmler mean anything to you?"

The college looks nearly empty as they walk up the sidewalk. But a few people are heading toward the largest brick building.

"Yes. A wife murderer. He was executed, right?"

"Indeed he was. He was an ax murderer actually. Terrible man. They put him to death after his trial. Upstate from here. Auburn Prison. First man ever killed by electrocution. At least the first one killed deliberately."

"Yes!" Victor remembers. "That was it! Ghastly death, right? Took them a few minutes to kill him, and they basically cooked the poor bastard." Victor stops and turns toward his friend, suddenly remembering the news. As he slowly recalls the details, he also remembers it struck him as very bad news the first time he heard it. "They used Westinghouse generators, didn't they? That's how they killed him. But we didn't supply them."

"No. It was an Edison deal, that bastard. He specifically had someone else buy the generators, then he provided them to the prison. He convinced them to use *our* generators just so he could stoke the bad publicity. He wanted to make sure it was alternating current that killed Kemmler!"

Tesla fumes. "Make AC look dangerous and deadly, that was his whole reason for getting involved. I hate Thomas Edison, the whore. I hate every whisker on his fat face. You know I do."

"Yes. I know, Nikola. And I know how he cheated you. But what does that have to do with Brown?"

"Think, boy! Edison's whole empire is built on direct current. But now we have developed a better system! People slowly are realizing that. Engineers looking to light up towns and build power plants—all of these smart men are slowly realizing that alternating current is a better solution for them. Edison owns very few patents for AC current. He has nothing that will make him anywhere near the money he's making from DC. So he's fighting for this any way he can. He is painting AC as more dangerous than DC. That's just one of his many tricks. And he has our dear Professor Brown in his back pocket, I'd say."

Victor reaches the steps to the building and turns to his friend and mentor. "So that's the man we're going to see. The man who's trying to destroy Westinghouse, your work. Our work. Why? Why grace him with your presence? You already know what he will say. People know you, Nikola. Many know why you left Edison to come to work for Westinghouse. People will see you here in the audience. I don't care if they *do* call him the wizard of Menlo Park. Edison is still trying to destroy us, and your attendance may actually look like support!"

"Does it? Well, Victor, you'll see why I'm going to this lecture. Not to show support, but to keep an eye on things. And maybe, just maybe, to ask some very public questions."

"Oh Nikola, no. This could get ...."

But Tesla just winks, and they head up the stairs.

Chapter 31

Elevation

Kansas City's Union Depot, at more than 350 feet in length, is a brute of a building. There are unmatched sets of lights here and there along its exterior walls. Some are electric and some gas. But the building still seems dark and castle-like. It rises out of a sandy plain and stands guard near the Kansas River.

Amanda notices the huge clock tower that looms over the entrance. There is a slight glow coming from the tower, and it helps illuminate the surrounding area.

Strangely, she feels none of the fretful worry that she felt when first pulling into New York. It's not just because Kansas seems to be a safer place. Amanda also feels more at ease with her travels now. She knows how train trips work, and she feels more at peace with the sheer adventure of it all.

Other trains are arriving. As she steps down from her grimy coach she has to shield her face from black coal smoke and the ever-present soot. This depot seems even more crowded and bustling than Chicago and New York. All the porters are busy. She lifts her own sack and turns sideways several times in order to squeeze through groups of travelers. Many of them stand lost and bewildered. Some argue amongst themselves, maps and train schedules in hand, luggage strewn about their feet. It seems like every person in America suddenly decided to head west at the same time, using Kansas City as a waypoint.

Inside the terminal, Amanda finds endless hallways and corners. The roofline looks like a series of steeples that quietly merge with the building's hulking mansard roof, giving the whole place a dark, Gothic ambiance. She wonders how many travelers this building has swallowed up and spat out again as they make their way back and forth across the country.

At least the main waiting area looks plush and comfortable. On one side are padded benches. On the other is a fine restaurant with white tablecloths and polished silverware. She finds herself cursing the place's pretentiousness while at the same time longing to sit there for a while, just to enjoy the luxury. But the money in her pocket won't fund such extravagance.

Amanda hoists her own tied tablecloth—her makeshift travel sack—over her shoulder and heads for the restrooms.

The ladies' room turns out to be a wondrous surprise. Despite the fact that it's built over creek waters—which simply wash away all public waste—the room itself seems luxurious. It's finished in strips of walnut, ash, and yellow pine. It offers dressing-room style seats mounted in metal posts. There are even tall water closets with long brass pull chains and hand-painted ceramic handles. Amanda washes her face in the sink and feels slightly guilty just for wetting the surface of the polished porcelain.

Back in the lobby, a manager in a blue uniform walks through the crowd, announcing the arrival of trains from Denver and St. Louis. The huge room suddenly whirs with activity. A woman stops the station manager to ask a question, and soon a small line forms behind her—other confused travels need help finding their way, too. The manager grows more irritable with each question.

Amanda has to get away from the bustle. Grabbing her sack, she walks through the front doors and trades one cacophony for another. Outside are the clatter of a streetcar and the shouts of cab drivers. Locals pull up in dusty wagons. The stench from sweaty, beshitted horses is insufferable. She heads up the street to escape it all.

In the distance, she sees something she's heard of, but not yet seen, either here or in Boston. It's an elevated railway that holds another streetcar. This one whizzes high above the people and the horse carts below. It's like a coach skimming through the air.

There's too much here to take in. The stir of an urgently growing city surrounds everyone. She hears hammering in at least four different directions. A wagonload of lumber heads up the street. A large yellow Labrador retriever stands guard on the wagon, tail wagging like mad, in the middle of the stack of boards.

Noticing a porter standing near the front curb, Amanda shows him a piece of paper. He smiles and points her toward a small building that sits near the edge of the rail yard. She has to backtrack a bit to get there.

"Around the corner and all the way to the back," he says. "You'll see it."

Once there, she walks through a door that says *yard manager* and finds an old man seated behind a desk. The only light comes from a railroad lantern sitting on a high shelf. Clearing her throat slightly, she waits for him to look up, then smiles.

"You must be Mr. Daniels."

He regards her without expression for several seconds, then nods, whispering, "Yeah, reckon I am." He seems to speak from only one corner of his mouth.

"I'm Amanda Grant. A gentleman in Chicago, by the name of Turner, suggested that I talk with you."

The man takes a filthy pipe from his lips and taps it gently, deliberately, into a makeshift ashtray in the middle of his green wooden desk. Amanda recognizes the container as a rounded white insulator that normally sits at the top of a telegraph pole.

"And why would Mr. Turner tell you to do that?"

She's taken aback, but smiles again. "Well, I guess because he considers you a friend. A union man. You are that, no?"

Yard Manager Daniels looks at her, admitting nothing.

"As is he," she continues.

"You union? Got a card?" he asks.

"No sir, I am not. There are not that many unions that include women. But Mr. Turner thought you could help me locate a friend of mine."

Silence.

"His name … is Jeb Thomas."

The old man nods, placing his pipe on the table.

"I may know the man," he declares, "but I don't know you. What's more, I don't know why I should help you or even trust you. Doesn't Mr. Turner know how to use a telegraph? He couldn't let me know you were coming?"

Amanda swallows hard. "Like I said. I'm a friend of his. Perhaps more than a friend, if that matters."

Mr. Daniels snorts. "A man like Jeb has a lot of women friends. Come to think of it, he has a lot of ex-friends too. But you probably know that. Who knows how those ex-friends feel about him? Might not be in his best interest or mine to help you find him, if you know what I mean."

He shakes his head. She's confused by this. What does he want? Money? Something else? She lacks experience in this kind of negotiation.

Amanda decides to look right back at him. "You know, sir, where I come from people simply help each other. It's what we do. It's the Christian approach to the world, is it not? Like I said, Jeb is a friend of mine. But I'm starting to wonder why, in his little corner of the world, everyone seems to think that's a problem."

"Ain't no problem yet, lady. You fixin' to make it one?"

"All I know is that everyone seems very suspicious of me and, it seems, suspicious of everyone else. Why is that, sir? Can you tell me?"

The old man smiles, nodding slightly as he pulls out a tobacco pouch. "A good Christian woman," he laughs. "That what you are?"

"Close enough." She looks out the window, hoping to spot someone else who might help her.

He shoots her an irritated glance, only to see her look back toward him then stare him down. Slowly he repacks his pipe. It takes three good puffs to get the embers glowing to the point where blue smoke trails up either side of his face. Shaking out the match, he finally grunts his agreement.

"Close enough? Okay. I guess that's fair. So let's test you and your Christian attitude then, shall we? Do you really want to know where Jeb Thomas is?"

"That's why I've come here."

"Well, from what I see, you've come here for help. His help. But what if it turns out that you're the one who will have to do the helping? Would that change things for ya? Or would that make you want to get on the next train and run away?"

"What do you mean, sir?"

"I mean that your friend ain't going to be very useful to you for a while, my dear. The fact is, I do know where Jeb is, so I'll tell ya. He's in jail. In jail with a black eye and a bloody nose to boot. Going to be there for a good long time, I'd say."

Amanda covers her face with her hands.

"I'm telling ya because I'd guess he can probably use a good woman right now, or any other friend that he can find." Mr. Daniels leans over his desk, lowering his voice a bit. "And, yes, his cause is my cause, too. You're right about that much. I could use a friend, too. We all could."

She shakes her head, unable to decide if she should cry or laugh at fate's cruel twists.

229

The man in the shack looks at her. "Do you think that's you, dearie? His friend in a time of need? Or does this change all your plans? Trains are leaving every fifteen minutes. You could be on any one of them."

Uninvited, she sits and slumps in the tiny office's only other chair.

Not knowing what to do with her, Daniels offers a cup of tea. They talk a bit, and he finally tells her how to find the jail. She can take the elevated train if she wants, and she decides to do just that.

Amanda feels exhausted and confused as she heads down the street. After a long trip, she wants only to find a bed for the night. But she must first find Jeb. He may need her.

She walks toward the elevated tracks, stopping at a small apothecary to buy a bag of lemon drops and a bottle of "Lydia Pinkham's Vegetable Compound" before climbing the platform to the train.

Chapter 32

Body Electric

Victor Marius and Nikola Tesla slip through the doors of the lecture hall and take seats near the back. The scene before them is surreal. Three people adorned in spotless white lab coats stand on the stage. They wear black rubber gloves and oversized goggles. It's more theater than science. The hall is nearly full, to the point where several people stand at the back and sides.

The place is wired for electricity, as are most of the buildings at the college. But the main overhead lights remain dark tonight. Instead, the stage is illuminated with a series of clear bulbs, each a fat six inches in diameter. They hang from a wire stretched across the middle of the stage. The wire is attached to one of two generators that sit at either side of the platform. Both generators are running, but only the one on the right is connected to the lights. The one on the left doesn't seem to be connected to anything. The generators are powered by gasoline and have long metal tubes attached to their sides to carry their exhaust gasses out the stage door.

Victor swings his eyepiece down to give him a closer look at the stage, then swings it away again.

The strangest sight is a large steel cage that stands near the right side of the stage. It contains two large German shepherds, one of whom paces nervously.

The lecture begins. Professor Brown, goggles pushed back onto the top of his head, starts with a brief history of electricity, explaining things like friction, lightning, and the conductive properties of various metals. He explains how the conductivity makes it possible to send electricity over wires. He then walks back and forth between the two generators, explaining how each works and what kind of power they produce.

The introduction is fairly basic. In several ways, the big units do similar jobs. They both produce electricity, which can be used to power electrical lights "just like the ones you see stretched over this stage," the professor says.

The talk goes on for several more minutes. He stops to take a few questions then begins a short segment on how the internal portions of the generators work. At one point, he produces a hand-cranked dynamo about the size of a shoebox. He calls about ten people out of the audience and asks them to hold hands as they form a semicircle.

"Here now!" he calls out in a loud voice. "You, and you!" He asks the person on each end of the semicircle to grasp a piece of metal that looks like the end of a child's jump rope. As he turns the crank, the group laughs and squeals, feeling a low level of electricity pass through their linked hands. He then places the two metal ends into a small metal dome, about a foot apart. He has a woman place her hand on the dome, and the audience laughs as her hair rises high.

"Party tricks," Nikola grumbles quietly. "You can see this act at circus sideshows."

After drawing some illustrations on a chalkboard about the nature of electrical circuits, Brown turns his attention to the units on the stage.

"Both of these generators are good ones," Brown explains. "Top of the line at the moment. They produce no odor, heat, or danger of fire." He steps to the forestage and drops his voice to a loud whisper, a showman taking the audience into his confidence. "By now, most of you probably have seen these types of circuits. Several buildings in this fair city of New York are already electrified. Yet most people don't know much about the vastly different types of electricity available to them. But I think it's very, very important that people *do* know. Yes, indeed I do. And you—the engineers, college students, professors, and concerned citizens attending this lecture—*you* can help people understand these differences."

Victor leans toward Tesla's ear. "This guy's good. Every eye in here is focused right on him."

Tesla bites his lower lip and nods.

"Now, you may ask why there are two generators here tonight," the professor shouts, fingers held high. His voice starts to take on the cadence of a revival preacher saving souls at a summer gospel tent. "And as you can see, they look roughly the same, but there are slight differences here at the front." He uses a long wooden dowel to point out the mechanical differences.

"This generator, here on the right, produces direct current. We call it DC. I'm sure many of you already know it's the absolute best system available for distributing electricity." There is a slight buzz in the audience. It's not clear if all attendees agree with the statement. Victor starts to raise his hand, ready to challenge it. Tesla pats his shoulder, urging him to wait.

The professor points to the other generator. "On the other hand, this particular generator over here, the one with the Westinghouse label on the front, produces alternating current, or AC. Now, I admit that AC does have some advantages over DC, but it also has many disadvantages. In general, it's good for carrying power over a great distance, but that means dangerous currents passing right through your neighborhood. And most but far more important, its structure makes it too dangerous for everyday use. Because of the way this generator produces power, it's too easy for someone to come in contact with it. If that happens, the results can be quite deadly."

"Nonsense!" came a shout, but not from Victor—from a young engineering student in the front row. "AC is perfectly safe, when handled correctly."

"Is that so?" Brown replies, looking over his glasses through the glare of the bulbs. "Then why have so many people been electrocuted coming into contact with AC current? There have been dozens of deaths to date, some right here in New York!"

"Some people have been killed by DC current, too!" he shouts back.

"Yes. Some. Not many though. And might I remind you that an AC generator," he points at the label, "a Westinghouse generator mind you, was used to execute the first prisoner ever killed by electricity. It happened right upstate from here. Those in charge apparently were well aware of the killing power of AC."

Background conversation in the hall rises to a loud buzz. Victor looks at Tesla. The older man holds up a finger again, urging patience.

Professor Brown's voice suddenly takes on a humble tone. "But you don't have to just take my word for it. I am here tonight not only to deliver a lecture on electricity, but to show you the difference, the dangerous difference, between the two different types of current."

The audience is silent as he points to the lights. "As you can see, we are illuminated tonight by the generator on the left. That's the one that produces direct current. I thought it would be safer to start there since these lights have been on for a couple hours now. But I can unplug the wires and attach them to the other generator whenever we need." To illustrate his point, Brown asks that the regular lights in the auditorium be brought up, and then he stops the generator and detaches the wires, which are held in place by a pair of clips. He then attaches the wires to the AC generator and starts it up. The stage lights start to glow again, and the house lights go back down.

"As you can see, the lights are lit once again. There is no noticeable difference in how they look." He holds his hands up near one of the globes. "This is an important point. Same light. Same heat. And if I may be so bold, the same service to the citizens of this fair city."

Brown makes a broad, showy gesture to the lights. "Look at them! The lights themselves don't care whether they are powered by AC or DC current. I'm willing to bet the people using the lights don't much care either. They just want their lights to work!" He smiles as if he's just touched on the main focus of his whole lecture.

"Lights please? Again?"

As the house lights brighten, he goes through the procedure again, reattaching the wires to the DC generator. Then he looks at the audience, his voice dropping low and loud, this time sounding like a carnival barker calling for men to come and visit a burlesque tent.

"So, you may ask, if it's the same light, if it's the same service to the masses, then why should we care about the difference at all? Why not allow each power company across the nation to choose their own system, and be happy with their own choices?"

He holds a finger up, like a powerful evangelist saving souls with his new machine. "I'll tell you why. Safety! That's the main reason, pure and simple! Safety for everyone."

Brown motions to his assistant, a young man with blond hair and a scruffy beard. The helper nods and walks to the dog cage. He opens it and takes one of the German Shepherds by its collar. There's a low "aww" from the audience as he walks the animal across the stage. It's only then that Victor and Tesla notice the dog is wearing a metal collar and a small metal bracelet on one of his back legs.

"He's not going to shock it?" Victor whispers to Tesla.

His friend remains silent.

The Shepherd wags his tail as Professor Brown takes charge of the dog and walks him to a platform. Two steps up and the dog sits back on his haunches. Brown pops a treat into the dog's mouth, then strokes him under his chin.

As the dog sits, Brown attaches one wire to the collar and another to the leg bracelet. The crowd leans forward.

"This little demonstration will show you something very important about DC current."

Walking back toward the generator, he stops at a tiny table. Two levers sit on the tabletop. "Right now, the wires connected to the dog are not conducting electricity. But when I throw this switch, it will send 110 volts of electricity though him, from neck to foot."

The audience starts to gasp, but he doesn't wait for the protests. Forcing the switch down, a jolt of electricity is sent through the dog who yelps, then visibly shivers. The animal slowly falls to its knees, a low, guttural growl coming from its clenched teeth. Ten seconds pass, then twenty. A woman screams. Several people in the audience stand up yelling for him to stop. The professor finally raises the lever, and the dog slouches low, panting and whining.

"As you can see, the animal was indeed shocked by the DC current. And I will admit that it was not comfortable for him. I do apologize for that. Yet this dog is still alive. The 110 volt jolt didn't kill him."

His assistant settles the dog. Brown walks away from his controls and lets his assistant take his place. The young man moves his hand to the other lever. "He'll be fine, by the way," Brown says loudly. "Later on I'll give him a nice steak dinner for his trouble." There are some snickers, and the whole audience seems to breathe a sigh of relief. Brown's other assistants retrieve the other dog from the cage. It growls and snaps at them as they tug it toward another platform. They produce a new set of wires and attach them to the collar and the foot, same as the other dog. But this time they attach the leads to the AC generator.

"Now, this time the switch will send the same amount of current through the dog," Professor Brown announces. "Again, it will be exactly 110 volts, just like the DC current."

He ignores a scream of "no" from the front of the room. He gives a nod to his blond assistant who slams the other lever down. The dog howls and writhes. Its gums pull back, freezing a ghastly, teeth-baring growl on its face. In ten seconds the big Shepherd stops shaking and becomes still as a statue, as if its feet are glued to the platform. A tuft of dog hair floats away. The smell of burnt meat hangs in the air. When the level finally is released, the dog falls over with a thud, like a dead bag of sand. There is silence in the room, broken only by the sound of a gaseous hiss that emanates from the rear of the lifeless dog.

The audience finally roars—all at once. Many are angry, while many others laugh, nervously, even callously, at what they've just witnessed. As someone shouts that the professor is a horse's ass, Brown slowly raises his hand, attempting to calm the masses.

"I know! I know! This is a ghastly business. I'm sorry. *Sorry*! All right?" he shouts. "But in the name of science, I hope that you can see that this was an important demonstration. It's no different from some of the other experiments on animals that take place right here at Columbia! No different from dissecting frogs or pigs in the name of science!"

The audience slowly quiets, and Brown once more tries on his confidential, mentoring voice. "I think you can see," he says as the assistants remove the dog carcass from the stage, "that this experiment drives home the very point I'm trying to stress. Do you see the danger that one type of current has, versus the other?"

"That dog did not need to die for you to make your point!" a young woman shouts.

"You've got that right," says the engineering student in the front.

"Please! Please! You have to understand! That dog, whom I rescued from certain death anyway in a dog pound, expired here tonight so that others might live! So that *people* might live!" He waves his pointing dowel at the group like he's casting a magic spell. "Every one of you in this room is in a position to make a difference. You can tell others about the dangers you've seen here! Tell them about the danger of AC current. Tell them what the safe choice is! More and more power companies are looking to use AC as a way to transmit electricity over distances. Why are they doing it? They're doing it to save money, my friends. They are willing to create dangerous power grids so that they don't have to build as many power stations. Yes, they save money, but at what cost to others? Whose need is more important? Are their finances more important than your safety? How about your family's safety?"

A murmur runs through the crowd. Professor Brown has hit a sweet spot, and he knows it. As he moves in for the hard sell, Tesla shifts in his seat. His knuckles whiten as he clenches his armrest.

"What I have come here tonight to stress," Brown continues, "is that there are far safer ways to illuminate cities and towns. Everyone needs to know this—especially you, the educated leaders of your communities. As electrical wires are extended into more and more neighborhoods—even your own neighborhoods—the problem, too, becomes your own."

Tesla whispers to Victor that they shouldn't be the first ones to try to ask a question. He wants to get a feel for the audience, to see where they stand on the issue. He also doesn't want to give Brown a chance to tell him to wait, that it's not time for questions yet. He won't let Brown take the upper hand in this important debate.

"My main message tonight," Brown lectures, "besides helping people understand electricity, is to tell citizens that they need to keep a careful watch on the companies who are now seeking to provide electricity to their neighborhoods. The competition is fierce right now. Everyone wants electricity, and many new companies want to grow rich by fulfilling that need. But where will the generating plants be located? How will the power come down those wires and into your houses? What kind of electricity will it be?" He gestures to the DC generator on the stage. "I propose to you that it's far safer to build smaller plants closer to your houses and businesses, rather than a few large plants designed to serve a full city. It may be cheaper for power companies to build centralized facilities, but it's more risky to you!"

There are nods of approval. Brown leans forward, whispering. "Can you be sure that your children will never come in contact with the electrical wires that eventually will come to your house? Are you willing to take that chance?"

Victor speaks softly to Tesla. "Smart approach. Make the AC folks look selfish, then make everyone else will feel like they're not doing their job if they don't try to stop them."

Tesla nods, scanning the crowd, waiting for the questions to begin. Brown ignores the raised hands for a while, then finally calls on a man who looks to be about thirty years old in the front row. The man doesn't appear to be a student, and as he talks, Victor and Nikola speculate that he may be a shill, planted there to ask some easy, supportive questions.

"You make some interesting points," the man begins. "So what can we do to help keep our families safe? Should we object to electrification of our homes and neighborhoods when the time comes?"

"Oh no, no, not at all." The professor laughs. "You'd be fighting a losing battle. And electrification offers far too many benefits. People want it in their homes, and that's understandable."

"Then what?" the man asks.

"Well, work with your local government. Work to be sure the right kind of power is brought in. Be safe and reasonable, and find a good local spot where a DC power plant can be located in your neighborhood."

A few more questions are asked, mostly about the technical differences between the two generator types. Tesla is worried that he might be recognized by Brown if he stands to ask a question, so he asks Victor to take the lead instead.

Victor agrees. "Just a simple question, sir," he says when he's finally called. "Has anyone ever been accidentally electrocuted by DC current?"

Brown is slow to answer. "Well, yes. Of course. I've already said that. Any industry has its accidents."

"And can you tell me what the voltage was for the accident?"

"I'm afraid I don't know that."

"I do. There was a person in this very city killed six months ago by sixty volts of DC current. I believe you just used 110 volts of AC to kill that dog."

The whole front part of the audience turns in unison to see who is talking. Victor smiles politely and watches Brown carefully.

"Perhaps, but the point is, young man, that both of these generators produced the exact same level of electricity tonight, 110 volts. You saw what happened to the first dog, and then the second. I admit, no electricity is 100 percent safe 100 percent of the time. All types must be handled carefully. But the difference here tonight was obvious. DC is simply safer. The dog survived. We all saw that."

Victor steps into the aisle, visibly challenging Brown. All eyes are on him. "Since no electricity is totally safe, then engineers and electricians such as you and I have to follow rules. We don't touch it directly. We insulate the wires as much as needed. We certainly insulate every contact point. The rules are not difficult ones. I think that if those rules are followed, it doesn't matter one bit what kind of current is in the wires. Likewise, if the rules are *not* followed, the people who touch the electricity are not safe. Period. Either type of electricity can kill if not handled correctly."

Brown squints at his questioner. "I'm afraid, sir, that people can't be trusted to never make such mistakes. You can't trust a child not to be curious." He wags his finger at Victor. "Also, part of the distribution method of AC power is the use of transformers. Safe, low-voltage AC current can be transformed into a very dangerous high-voltage supply at local substations, and vice versa. This method shows no regard for the safety of the local population. The safer DC solution is simply the better one."

Tesla doesn't stand, but his loud voice and heavy Croatian accent fill the room. "It's especially the better solution for those who sell the DC generators, such as yourself, no?"

There is dead silence in the hall. Brown's face grows red, not with embarrassment, but with anger. "Excuse me? I don't know what you're talking about."

Tesla slowly stands. There are whispers in the crowd, mostly from the engineering students who recognize him. Many have studied his theories and patents. "Then I apologize for not choosing my words carefully enough. I don't claim that you yourself are selling generators. But I do believe you are working directly for Mr. Edison, no?"

Brown walks right to the edge of the stage, looking down on the crowd. "I work for no one, Mr. Tesla. That's who you are, correct? Nikola Tesla? I recognize you, sir, and I very much resent what you are saying. I am an independent professor and researcher—much as yourself. I understand also that you are no longer working directly for the Westinghouse Company at the moment. Is that true?"

Tesla nods. "It is."

"Then I guess I should ask you the same thing. Are you an independent researcher who was paid by Westinghouse to come here tonight and challenge me?"

"No, I am not. I live nearby. I came out of curiosity. But please, since we're on the subject, tell me who paid for *your* travel here. Who gave you the generators, and who pays to ship these heavy things all around the country, to all your speaking engagements? For that matter, who uses his connections and calls in favors to arrange speaking engagements for you at universities and, dare we admit it, county fairs? Would Columbia ever have invited you, *Professor* Brown, to speak here without that quiet influence?"

Brown abruptly calls on another person. The debate is over, but Tesla's point has been made. As the lecture breaks up, several young students come over to Tesla, eager to meet him. Victor can see that the fawning attention makes the man proud, and it temporarily eases the anger he saw lurking beneath Tesla's surface. Brown packs up and leaves, making no effort to greet the two of them personally.

Chapter 33

Shadows

The quick glint of metal from the policeman's badge is difficult to see in darkness of the park.

Gaslights line the two main paths through the public spaces of Boston Common, but they don't cast their glow more than thirty feet. Beyond that there is mottled gray. People lurk in those shadows, including the owner of the badge.

The benches he passes either sit empty, or they're occupied by forlorn alcoholics or aging homosexual men who seek relief from their temporary desperations.

"Move along, you!" the policeman says. A thin man scurries away, never fully seen by anyone.

The patrol, such as it is, is only a ruse. It gives the policeman an excuse to be here. One of the lurking men could mean a bit of money to him. Side money. Money to which he feels entitled, given all the risks, day in and day out, that are taken by a man who stands behind a badge.

The policeman walks toward the Beacon Street side of the park. About 100 feet ahead of him, he sees a man light a cigarette. The policeman approaches. He draws close enough that the smoker is able to see that he's a cop, but he doesn't budge. Instead he awaits for the policeman's arrival.

"That you?" the cop asks as he approaches.

"I suppose it's me, yeah," Devlin Richards responds. "Nice to see you again. I think."

The officer walks up beside him. "So Chen Lu's lawyer friend says I should talk to you."

"This place gives me the creeps," Devlin says. "Don't know why you want to meet here."

"Let's just say it's a good place to not be noticed," the officer smirks. "Lot of these losers would agree."

But in Devlin's mind, this is an evil place. It's evidence of the depraved Yankee lifestyle and their willingness to tolerate just about anything. He'd just as soon see the world rid of such people.

The police officer gets down to business. Reaching into his coat, he pulls out a dark paper bag. "Before we talk about our other business, I want you to take a look at this. Think you can sell it?" He opens up a brown bag and lets Devlin take a look inside.

Devlin's eyes widen at what he sees. "Well, fuck the dog. Ain't that a lot of stuff! Who did you take that from?"

"It's probably not what you think," the cop says, slowly unfolding the top of the sack. "It ain't poppy juice. This here's something different."

He reaches in and pulls out a handful of loose greenish-brown vegetation that looks to Devlin like a combination of dried broccoli and pencil shavings.

"Apparently this sort of stuff has been making its way around the city for a while," the cop continues, "but I don't hardly ever see it. This is only the second time I've confiscated this sort of thing. Took it off a piano player at one of them nigger clubs, you know, down south side."

Devlin looks closer. "What the hell is it?"

"They call it bhang. Got some other names, too. Comes up from the South. They says it's usually used to make rope."

"So what do you do with it, eat it?"

"No, no, they smoke it, just like opium. I seen them do it out behind the club. They roll it into cigarettes or pack it down into a pipe and then they pass it around. 'Bhanging it,' they say. Easy way to make an arrest for a cop. Just go down there and look. "

"They play that damn bone-jarring music with the piano and sometimes some horns. That noise don't make a lick of sense to me. But when the bands take their breaks, everyone wanders outside, still dancing and shuffling around. I just have to watch from a distance. Someone will light up eventually. Then I move in."

Devlin nods toward the bag. "Laws against it?"

"Hell no. Law don't even know what this stuff is. But I keep what I take off anyone that I hassle. Makes them think twice if they see me coming again. That's how I like it, and that's how I got this here load. Guy was disturbing the peace. I told him so."

"That a fact?"

The cop laughs, and Devlin waves the bag away. "I've got no market for that. Wouldn't even know who to sell it to."

"Sell it back to one of them! Jesus, I'll tell you where all the clubs are."

"And you say there's buyers?"

"All sorts of 'em. But I can't sell it. Cop can't be seen doing that."

"How much they pay for something like that?"

"Ahh, who knows? A few bucks. We split the money and I'll find you some more."

Devlin takes the bag and looks inside. "Doesn't make any sense. Stuff feels kind of bulky, like it should be on a salad. Hard to carry around compared to opium."

"No more bulky than tobacco really."

Devlin shrugs. "I guess I can give it a shot. But since I have no idea what it sells for, you'll have to spot me on it. I'll pay you half of whatever I get."

The cop sighs. "Yeah, all right. I suppose we can do that. Didn't pay nothing for it in the first place."

Devlin stashes the bag in his coat, looking around to see who might be near.

"Now it's your turn," the cop says. "Tell me why you wanted to meet."

Devlin looks around again. "I wanted to ask you about something that's sitting in your evidence room."

The cop shakes his head. "Oh no. Disappearing evidence? That's never a good idea. Sorry."

"Look, I'm doing you a favor with the drug, right? I need a favor, too. This is a big one."

"I get caught for something like that, it's my badge. I'm only a few years from retirement. Forget it."

Devlin bites his tongue for a moment, then gives the other man a sideways glance. "So I guess twenty-five dollars doesn't get your attention."

"What? How much?"

"You heard me."

"What the hell do you want out of the evidence room that's worth twenty-five dollars?"

"Just a stupid wooden box. No big deal."

The cop shakes his head. "How can a wooden box be worth that much money?"

"I'm not even sure that it is. Just a bit of a gamble. Owner's gone anyway. Out of town, probably for good."

The policeman looks at the sky, weighing his options. "Just a wooden box, you say."

"Size of a shoebox, give or take."

The cop is silent.

"I can give you a full description. Draw a little sketch, if that would help."

"Well, I suppose it can't hurt just to look. No promises, though."

"I know. Just take a look around. Tell me if it's there. We can decide then."

"You drive a hard bargain, sir. You know that?"

Devlin nods. "It's business. What can I say?"

Chapter 34

Elixir

As the crowd wanes, Tesla and Victor walk to the street and hail a hansom cab to head back toward Tesla's neighborhood. Each sits lost in his own thoughts as they jostle over the uneven streets.

It's obvious to Victor that the ongoing and very public argument with Edison is taxing to Tesla. A raw anger seethes and boils inside him, to the point where Victor worries about his mentor's mental state.

The cab lets them off at the curb, but before returning home, Victor suggests they stop at a small pub to indulge in a glass of absinthe. A waitress in a low-cut dress ushers them through the crowd to a table near the rear. Once seated, they smoke, make small talk, and drink a beer. As the absinthe tray arrives, they perform a ritual of preparation that's unique to those who know the drink well. It's a very formal process—the ice, the strainer, the light green smoke—and going through the motions seems to add to the power of the exotic drink.

They sip slowly, and after about twenty minutes, the greenish liquid seems to amplify all of Tesla's hidden obsessions. He spends the next hour scribbling charts on the edges of old newspapers, all the while ranting about Edison.

Victor tries to calm him, and after the Croatian has said his piece, his sketches change a bit. His drawings start to focus on things other than electricity.

"Electricity as a new technology is moot at this point now, you know that," Tesla says. "Most of the big research is done. It's already a commodity business. We manufacture the generators, and fledgling power companies come to us, buy them, and install them all over the map. Edison is worried while George Westinghouse seems perfectly happy with the arrangement, even as Edison tries to push him out of the market. Westinghouse is still making a fortune. And that's the problem."

"What do you mean?"

"I mean George knows he has a winning formula, and he doesn't want to change it. He doesn't seem to want to branch out. It's a gravy train, and he doesn't seem to see the looming threats."

"And you do, I take it?"

"Yes. I do. Just like you do, Victor. You saw the shit show tonight."

They sit in silence for a moment.

"And radio, too. That could be the next big thing on the horizon, if it can be sorted out. Right? Isn't that what we both believe? But George won't invest in radio. I don't know if he doesn't think it's possible, or if he just doesn't care because he has other things to worry about."

Victor shrugs. "Radio could turn out to be little more than a dream, Nikola. It's not at all clear how money will be made from it. I can certainly understand why Westinghouse doesn't want to sink many resources into it."

"Oh no. It's more than just a dream, my friend. You wouldn't have been out on the water doing your tests if it was just a dream, would you?"

Victor suddenly feels lightheaded from sipping the drink. Absinthe provides a far different sort of intoxication than other liquors. He's never quite developed a taste for it but finds it fun to experience the dizzy fog now and then.

"Is that why you've decided to go off on your own for a while?" Victor asks. "To pursue radio research?"

"Yes. Well, maybe. Yes and no."

Tesla orders them two more absinthes. Victor isn't at all sure that's a good idea and says so. He sees how the liquid affects Tesla. Pupils dilated. His usual nervous energy somehow soothed to a mumbling bounce. But the waitress shushes Victor and goes to bring more drinks.

She returns with the standard absinthe arrangement: two tall tumblers that look like parfait glasses from an ice cream shop, but not quite as wide at the top. Inside each tumbler sits two inches of nearly clear liquid. She places a trowel-shaped spoon across the rim of each tumbler and perches cubes of sugar on each spoon. She gives the men a small pitcher of ice water. Tesla dribbles the water over each of the spoons, watching the sugar cubes slowly dissolve into the glasses. The clear absinthe turns opalescent green as the last of the cold sugar water trickles into the glasses. Each man picks up a spoon and swirls his drink then taps his spoon on the rim, completing the peculiar drinking ritual.

Victor sips and continues. "So you believe there's some new kind of fortune to be made in radio? All right, let's say

I agree. Even though I'm starting to wonder if I'll ever be part of it."

"Oh, it's much more than just the fortune," Tesla confides. "I've been thinking long and hard these late nights while working in my lab, Victor. Let me show you something."

He draws another sketch. This time it's of a large steel tower. Tesla explains that a full-size version would be higher than France's two-year-old Eiffel Tower. It would have a huge steel-mesh ball on top and a huge generator at its base. A motor would drive a large rotating coil inside the ball.

"This design would be far different from the coils we've built so far. I don't have a clear design for it yet," he says, fingers dangling over the sketch, "but the basic idea is in my head. I know I can generate a tremendously strong signal. Much stronger than mere radio waves. It's just a matter of building the system. Trust me, it would be incredibly powerful."

"How so? What would it be used for?"

"To get rid of the wires, boy. To get rid of the wires for everything! That's where we're going eventually. Don't you think all of this expensive stringing of wires is just going down the wrong path?" He laughs as he sees Victor frown.

"The wires are just making the copper miners rich—that's all. I consider them a temporary solution. This radio you and I are working on, Victor, it's not just about communicating with ships out at sea. Properly configured, it's about moving everything." Tesla gestures broadly with his hands, his absinthe-slurred voice loud enough to draw stares from others. "Radio is about sending signals. Dots and dashes at first, but it could be used for sending voices, too. That's where you want to go, right?"

Victor nods.

"Well, what if I told you that I have a design that could send not only voices out over the horizon, but pictures, too? How would that strike your fancy?"

Victor raises an eyebrow. "I guess I'd be intrigued, Nikola. Skeptical, but intrigued."

"What if I said I could do even more? What if I could send electricity itself through the air? Make it hop from tower to tower. What if I could send power to any place in the globe where it was needed, and what if I could do it without wires?"

Victor looks his friend and mentor in the eye. "I'd say you were mad."

"Ha! Mad! Yes!" Tesla slams his hand down on the table. "That's indeed what many will say. But I can do it, you know! I absolutely *know* that I can."

He leans forward, eyes wild and unfocused. "Do you remember how many people said I was mad when I had the idea for alternating current? But I did it, didn't I? I showed them it could be done, and Goddamn it, it's going to be the winning technology, in spite of Edison and killer clowns. AC is the power grid of the future. You *know* I won!"

Victor smiles but waves off the waitress as she approaches for another drink order. No more of the cursed green drink. It brings out a side of Tesla that Victor doesn't like. The man may be a genius, but there has always lurked a certain lunacy beneath his genius.

Tesla excuses himself and goes to the water closet. Victor stares at the remaining witch's brew of liquid in their glasses. Absinthe is the drink of artists. It's the conduit of visions and the soother of troubled creative souls. Can an engineer also become a conduit for creative visions when drinking the stuff? Or does it make him think too much, to the point where he becomes troubled and lost in a jumble of competing images and thoughts?

Victor reaches beneath the table and pours most of what's left in both glasses onto the floor just as Tesla returns.

"You know, when I was in England, I drank a lot of this stuff," Victor says with a smile. "Every once in a while there would be editorials in the papers there, deriding absinthe as a grave danger. They say it punches permanent holes in one's intellect."

Tesla grunts his indifference.

"One story that I particularly remember quoted Oscar Wilde."

"Wilde? Who's he? Never heard of him."

"Irish playwright and author. He's more famous over there than he is here."

Tesla shrugs. Victor holds the glass up to a light, looking through the last remaining drops at the bottom.

"*The drink* is all they call it over there. Anyway, the article quoted Wilde as saying, 'After the first glass you see things as you wish they were. After the second, you see things as they are not.'"

"Then perhaps we should drink three!" Tesla slurs.

"Oh no, just listen to this. Wilde went on to say that after three: 'Finally you see things as they really are, and that is the most horrible thing in the world.'" Victor puts the glass down and looks Tesla in the eyes.

"You are a driven man, my friend. I worry that you are driving yourself too hard."

"Perhaps," the older man nods. "But what of you? You look as old, if not older than me right now. You look tired, too."

"Yes, well ...." Victor looks down at the tabletop. Indeed. What of him? A man with arm and chest braces made of leather and scrap metal. Who is he to lecture the great Nikola Tesla? Tesla finally found the fortune that eluded him when he worked with Edison, and now he's off on some new adventure with a promise of even greater riches.

In contrast, Victor isn't working at all. The last thing he should be doing is chiding others about their shortcomings.

After they pay their tab, Victor walks Tesla home and sees that he goes to bed.

On his own way home, he laments that his friend, the only real colleague he has at the moment, is showing signs of instability. He's not sure if he feels worse for Tesla or for himself. If Tesla can lose himself in wishful dreams, it seems that anyone can.

So, what of Victor Marius. Wasn't that the pending question? Are his dreams worth pursuing? Or is he equally mad just for dreaming at all?

Chapter 35

Injection

A few hours later, Victor finds himself on a train from New York, heading back toward Boston. His time with Tesla was interesting, but he's not sure what to make of it.

This is a late-night trip. The cars are quiet as the locomotive pulls them through central Connecticut. Yet, he's restlessly walked the entire length of the train. Only about a dozen people are on board and most of them are fast asleep.

Victor's restlessness increases, and he's not sure why. He should be tired from his trip. He also should be tired from the absinthe he consumed. Yet, here he is. Eyes wide open. Pacing. Edgy.

Shaking off the unease, he slips into the train's commode. Even though this is a nice and relatively new car, the facilities seem like barely more than an outhouse. Flush the toilet and it just dumps out onto the tracks. You can see railroad ties speeding below the hole.

Victor takes out his syringe. Finds a good muscle. Avoids the veins. So much easier now that the doctor lets him do his own injections. His elixir goes in smoothly. And it now has just a hint of opium mixed in because he's found injecting it along with the mixture to be easier than separately smoking the white paste. The burn seems reduced when he injects. Or maybe he's just grown used to it.

The train lurches around a curve, and he widens his stance, closing his eyes and feeling himself vibrate along with every shift of the car.

Nice. Solid. Flying.

Heading back to his seat, Victor absentmindedly flexes his arms. He feels good. *His body* feels good. Muscles continue to grow bigger and stronger with each passing day. He's waited for this. Dr. Burke's sterol alcohol compound really has helped bring him back to health. And it seems the special opium-augmented concoction that Victor has created for himself also helps him deal with the pain. The lingering aches from the cuts and torn muscles. The fatigue from having to keep his eye focused, even when he uses the professor's special lens.

All of it, now, muted. Much easier to ignore.

He elects to walk on past his seat, figuring he'll stretch his legs a little more. Still pumping his arms a bit as he walks through the darkened cars, he heads toward the caboose.

As he steps through the rear door of the second-to-last passenger car, he notices a man outside on the small platform. He leans against the rail and smokes a fat cigar. The two men give each other a brief nod, and Victor heads on into the next car.

Something seems familiar about the smoker. It takes Victor a moment to realize where he's seen the man before. By the time he reaches the end of the aisle on the very last car the memory solidifies.

Yes. Even through his haze of opioid indolence, Victor recalls the man, where he saw him and what he did.

It was him. The one from the stage during the electrical demonstration. The young man with the blond hair who helped handle the dogs. He was the one who pulled the lever that made the kill.

Victor feels his fist tighten. But he forces himself to relax. He's not sure what to do, but he feels compelled to go talk to him. Taking a few deep breaths, he turns about, heads back outside and joins him on the small platform between the cars.

The nod to each other again.

"Nice night, eh?" Victor observes.

"Indeed. I had to come out to see the moon. Everyone else is asleep and missing it."

Victor stokes his chin. "So where are you from?"

They exchange quick pleasantries. Victor learns that man is just 20 years old. He's a university student on summer break. He's found work traveling up and down the East Coast, stopping at various cities to help with Brown's electrical demonstrations. They'll be heading to Chicago soon. The lad obviously is excited about having the chance to see that part of the country.

"So, I've heard of these shows," Victor lets on. "They talk about different types of electricity, right?"

"Different types of current. Yes. Direct Current is by far the best. The man I work for, Professor Brown, makes a very compelling case for that."

"I see," says Victor. "And how does he tell the story?"

"Well, it's easy to tell. AC is a killer. We certainly show that. It's dangerous stuff. It should never be used anywhere."

"Is that a fact?"

"Oh yes. When we go to the bigger cities, we show exactly how. I mean, it's not pretty. We've electrocuted dogs, goats. Even an elephant one time. The audience tends to get upset. But that's kind of the point. It's a great way to drive home the dangers."

Victor feels his fist tighten again. It's a strange feeling. It's not the haze of the opium that's driving the emotion. It's something deeper. Something primal that he doesn't quite understand, yet he's glad for the feeling. Empowered by it. He looks the young man in the eyes.

"You know, I probably should tell you. I have an interest in electricity myself."

The lad chuckles. "Seems like everyone does these days. It's a hot topic. It's an exploding technology and a great market for me to get involved in while I'm still a student." He takes a satisfied drag on his cigar and blows the smoke toward the moon. "I love being part of it."

Victor agrees that it's a rapidly growing field. "And I also should tell you, I was in the audience tonight. At your show. I saw the whole sordid lecture."

The man doesn't look worried. He actually looks pleased. Like he's found a kindred spirit. "That's wonderful! What did you think?"

The train whistle sounds as they crest a hill. The downward slope increases their speed. The cars shift. Victor hears the brakes tighten just a bit along the train's connections, slowing their descent. As they round a gentle curve along the side of a slope, he can see water in the distance, probably the Housatonic River.

"Hum… what did I think? Well, let me just say I disagreed with parts of it."

"Oh Jesus, don't tell me you're a Westinghouse fan. Those folks, I don't know…"

"No, no. Well," Victor holds up a finger, "I guess I do have some issues with your chosen current. But that's not really the main thing."

Victor shifts his weight a bit. Places his foot against the base of an upright steel bar that supports the platform's railing.

"Oh? Something else?"

Victor nods. Knowing he can be seen fairly well in the moonlight.

They're both silent for a moment.

"All right…" the lad takes another puff, then looks toward Victor. "Care to enlighten me?"

"You killed a fucking dog. That's what else."

The young man shrugs. "Yeah. Guess we did. So what? It's a dog. We got it from the pound."

Victor closes his eyes. Takes a breath, then grabs the other man by the collar, slamming him against the side of the car. The student's reaction is swift. At first he tries to push Victor's hands away, and when that proves difficult, he takes a swing at the dead center of Victor's face. But Victor blocks the blow, still managing to keep the man in place with just his left hand. "We're all dogs, aren't we? All one step away from the fucking pound. And we all deserve better than being used like that."

"What the hell?" the younger man demands. "Unhand me right now!"

Victor gives him a cold stare. "I don't know what angers me more. Watching you kill that dog, or telling lies about why you did it. Watching you shock the other one, too. It all made me furious. You know that? Furious." He takes a deep breath. "Silly, isn't it? I mean, I've gone hunting on occasion. I worked on a farm as a boy and watched animals live and die. But the certain callousness that you folks had. I don't know. That was something else entirely."

The student struggles and takes another swing. Victor responds with a quick uppercut to his jaw. The man winces and stops.

"But you know, lad, you know... I might have been able to forgive that. Once in a while things do end up dying in the interest of science, and we all accept that. It can be a nasty business. But we live with it. Only because it helps push us all forward."

He feels the train gain more speed as it reaches a halfway point down the hill.

"But what you all presented this evening was faulty science. It was a lie set up to promote Brown and Edison's selfish commerce. And I think bullshit is a lousy reason to kill. And when you kill an animal, and try to present your lie as some sort of important principal, well, that just...."

Victor seethes, takes a deep breath, then hisses through his teeth. "I do not intend to ride the same train as you. And I'm sure as hell not going to be the one who gets off."

The lad struggles and kicks. "You're crazy. Help!"

263

Victor leans toward his ear. "I'll give you one choice. The ground or the river?"

"What?"

"You heard me. Should I toss you now? Or should we wait for the river. It will be coming up soon. You'd better hurry."

The man kicks harder. Victor hoists him up onto his shoulder, then presses upward, lifting the man like a heavy bale of hay.

"No! Stop!"

"Not going to choose?"

Victor hesitates. He wants to throw him now. Maybe he will. But he looks toward the river—fast approaching.

"Guess I'll choose for you. And I'm feeling more humane than I should." The train speeds onto the trestle. There's dark water below. With a grunt and a mighty heave, he throws hard. And he does it with a final shout. "You'll live. Unlike that dog!" Then he laughs. "Well, as long as you can swim."

The man's cry is drowned out by the chug of the train and the rattle of the bridge. Victor watches the young man fall and barely clear the edge of the tracks. He twists and cartwheels toward the water. Victor anticipates and then imagines the splash even though he can't hear it.

At his feet, rolling slightly, lies the man's lit cigar. Victor picks it up before it can roll off the deck.

He takes a long puff, leans against the rail, and watches the trees rush by. It's a good cigar. Full. Rich.

Slowly, the train makes its way back up the far hill, and out of the river valley.

Chapter 36

Cell #118

Clank of metal in a dim hallway. Footsteps approach. Eyes slowly open.

He listens.

Two sets of footsteps this time, coming toward him.

Jeb Thomas sits up, looking through the bars as two figures stop at his cell door.

"Know this woman?" the guard grunts.

Jeb nods yes.

The night is dark, but thanks to dim light from a tallow candle, Amanda can see Jeb sitting on his bunk.

"Five minutes," the guard grunts again. "And keep yourself back from the cell, lady. I see you touching him or touching the bars and you're done, understand?"

Amanda nods and the guard walks about twelve feet away. He leans against the wall, lights a cigarette, and then nearly disappears as the match goes out. They only sense his presence by the arc of the glowing ember each time he raises the cigarette to his lips.

"Oh Jeb …," she nearly weeps, biting the knuckle of her index finger. He is quite a sight. A white bandage stretches across his nose but does little to hide a purple bruise beneath. Both eyes are bruised, too, not quite black, but bad enough to look purple and puffy. A crusty red and yellow scratch stretches the length of his cheek.

"What happened?"

"Oh, you know. How did you find me?"

"It wasn't hard. I only had to ask. Oh Jeb, what did they do to you?"

He grinds his teeth and looks away from her. "They were waiting for us. I don't know how, but they already knew. I just made it into town."

"Who was waiting?"

"Doesn't matter. 'Them' is just them. 'Them' is always one or more rough guys hired by the business owners who don't want any sort of union. They find dimwitted brutes who can be bribed for just a few dollars and some beer. Their only job is to see to it that men like me never make it to their scheduled meetings and rallies."

He coughs twice then holds his ribs in pain.

"But how did you end up in jail?"

"Because I started it."

"You what?"

"No, no ... I didn't really start the fight. I'd never start a fight, because it gets me nowhere. But that's the story that was told when the police showed up. And there were a handful of witnesses willing to back up the account, even though I don't remember seeing them. That's what the papers ended up reporting. *Labor troublemaker* comes to town. *Socialist revolutionary and agitator* stirs up trouble and gets violent when he's asked to leave. It's how they always paint me. Violent socialist. It's pretty easy to make me look like the bad guy if they want to."

"Oh Jeb …." She finally lets herself weep. She holds her head in her hands and cries for him, for the unfairness of the world, and maybe for herself, too. The guard looks on with distain.

Other thoughts rush to mind, too. Why has she fallen for a man who lives this kind of life? What kind of twisted world has she joined? This life of adventure to which she's so recently found herself attracted has revealed its harsh downside. She suddenly pines for her simpler life. A quiet, normal existence. But it's far out of reach. Will she ever see it again?

"What can I do?" Amanda asks in a quivering voice.

"I understand there's a labor lawyer in town. He knows of my situation here, yet he hasn't visited or sent word yet. I'm starting to worry."

"I'll find him for you."

"Can you?"

"You know I will." She starts to reach out to him, but the guard clears his throat and she drops her hand to her side.

"Thanks." Jeb smiles. "I wish I could hold you. I wish we were back in Boston. Maybe soon we can go back." Then he tells her the attorney's name and where he can be found.

"I'll try to find him first thing in the morning, Jeb. And a doctor? Do you need a doctor, too?"

The guard flicks his butt away, and it bounces down the hallway with a flicker of sparks.

"Start with the lawyer," Jeb says. "Then ask him if he can recommend a doc. They had one come in to see me yesterday, but I don't think he gives a damn if I live or die."

She nods then walks out of the building with the guard at her heels. It's after 9:00 p.m. She can't believe how much her world has changed since dawn.

End of Book 3

The Puzzle Box Chronicles is a series, starting with
Book 1
Wreck of the Gossamer.

* * *

*

The Story of Amanda, Jeb, Wayne, Victor, Devlin and
others continues in

The Lost, the Found and the Hidden
The Puzzle Box Chronicles: Book 2

Those Who Wander
The Puzzle Box Chronicles: Book 3

Wires and Wings
The Puzzle Box Chronicles: Book 4

North of Angel Falls
The Puzzle Box Chronicles: Book 5

Deep in a Box of Waves
The Puzzle Box Chronicles: Book 6